Gandhian Ideology and the Indian Novel

CHAMAN NAHAL'S *The Gandhi Quartet*

Gandhian Ideology and the Indian Novel

CHAMAN NAHAL'S

The Gandhi Quartet

A.V. SUBBA RAYUDU

PRESTIGE

Published by
PRESTIGE BOOKS
3/28, East Patel Nagar
New Delhi 110 008

2000

ISBN: 81-7551-075-7

Composed by Vivek Mathur, Delhi 110 006 Ph. 3981867
Printed by Dhawan Industries Offset, New Delhi 110 028

Contents

for

Professor K. Venkata Reddy
who is always inspired and inspiring

and

V.S. Ramachandra Rao
for his fruitful disagreement and
agreeable fruits of arguments

Preface

The novels of Chaman Nahal, in general, and his magnum opus, *The Gandhi Quartet,* in particular, have not received the critical attention they deserve. Barring a few articles in literary journals and books, there has been no full-length study of Nahal's fiction. We are yet to have a comprehensive book, assessing Nahal as a novelist.

The present book aims at making an indepth study of *The Gandhi Quartet,* which, almost like an epic, covers nearly four decades of India's history from 1915 to 1952, running into 2000 pages, portraying nearly 200 characters who belong to several ethnic groups, with its setting stretching from the Punjab to the Andamans and, above all, dealing with the enigmatic personality of Gandhi. It is hoped that a critical analysis of *The Gandhi Quartet,* the most extensive commonwealth novel, in terms of its themes and techniques, would help gain fresh insights into Nahal's fictional art.

The book is divided into seven chapters. The introductory chapter gives a brief account of Gandhian ideology, bringing out the image of Gandhi in the pre- and post-Independence Indian English fiction.

The next chapter is concerned with *The Crown and the Loincloth,* Volume 1 of *The Gandhi Quartet,* which describes how Gandhi revitalizes the slumbering spirit of the Indians and opens their eyes to the need and effectiveness of fighting the British government unitedly, thereby establishing Gandhi as a leader of the masses, par excellence.

The third chapter is about *The Salt of Life,* volume 2 of *The Gandhi Quartet*, which delineates Gandhi's historic march to Dandi, revealing as it does Gandhi's deep concern for his followers, including women, and his unflinching faith in them.

The fourth chapter concerns itself with *The Triumph of the Tricolour,* Volume 3 of *The Gandhi Quartet,* which shows how people respond to Gandhi's call for the Quit India movement, laying bare Gandhi's firm belief in the ultimate success of non-violent struggle for freedom, as also his frustration over the division of people on the basis of religion, caste, and creed.

The fifth chapter presents a critical analysis of *Azadi*, Volume 4 of *The Gandhi Quartet,* which shows how the dawn of freedom becomes a nightmarish and horrendous experience because of the holocaust of communal violence, driving home, at the same time, the need for religious harmony.

The penultimate chapter is concerned with the far-reaching significance of the "Epilogue," added to *Azadi,* which, besides linking together all the four volumes of *The Gandhi Quartet*, highlights the relevance of Gandhi to modern times.

The concluding chapter, while offering a summing up of the main argument of the book, seeks to assess the achievement of Nahal as a historical novelist.

II

I am grateful to Professor K. Venkata Reddy, Head, Department of English and Principal, S.K. University College, Anantapur, who initiated me into Nahal's fiction. His fund of scholarship, experience and critical acumen coupled with the filial affection, with which he and his wife, Dr. N.E. Bhagyavathy, treated me, have been the major sources of inspiration to me.

I also owe a debt of gratitude to Dr. K. Malakondaiah, Reader and Head, Department of Instrumentation, Dr. M. Chandraiah Chowdary, Professor of Chemistry, and D.P. Mallikarjuna Reddy, Reader in Physics, V.R. College, Nellore, for their moral and material support. Sri V.S. Ramachandra Rao and Sri T.B Rama Murti, retired lecturers in English, V.R. College, Nellore, with their loving care and sustained interest in my work, were an unfailing source of encouragement to me.

A.V. SUBBA RAYUDU

Introduction

The nation-wide Indian struggle for Independence was essentially an epic struggle, covering almost a century. The winds of change blowing steadily across the Indian subcontinent, after 'Sepoy' Mutiny in 1857, had left tell-tale marks on the political and social geography of the country. The Indian nation had to shake off the lethargy of the centuries, sink its religious, caste and provincial differences and march ahead on the road of progress. This was made possible only when the Gandhian whirlwind began to sweep over the length and breadth of India, upsetting all the established political and social strategies and ushering in refreshingly new ideas and methods. In the words of Jawaharlal Nehru: "Gandhi . . . was like a powerful current of fresh air that made us stretch ourselves and take deep breaths."[1] Gandhi was a politician, philosopher, social reformer, journalist and saint—all rolled into one. With the weapons of truth and non-violence, he inspired the entire nation with patriotism and idealism.

Mahatma Gandhi's relentless struggle for freedom has significant milestones like the non-violent non-cooperation movement of 1920-22, civil disobedience movement of 1930-31 and the Quit India movement of 1942. The non-violent non-cooperation movement created an unprecedented awakening, converting Indian nationalism from "middle class movement to a mass emotion." As R.C. Majumdar observes, the movement proved itself to be "a baptism of fire which initiated the people into a new faith and new hope, and inspired them with a new confidence in their power to fight for freedom."[2] The civil disobedience movement differed substantially from the non-violent non-cooperation movement, though the goal remained the same.

While the former hoped to bring the British government to a standstill by withdrawing from the administration, the latter sought to paralyze the government by mass performance of specific illegal acts. The Quit India movement led to violent underground revolutionary activity while Gandhi and his lieutenants languished in jail. Thus, the entire period of the Gandhian age was one of most far-reaching change, not only in the political scene but in practically all areas of Indian life.

It is but natural that these movements, which caught the imagination of the entire nation, inspired the Indian writers, particularly the novelists, and kindled their creative spirit. As Walter Allen has aptly put it: "In the literature of an age, its conflict, tendencies, and obsessions are uncovered and made manifest to a degree which is continually astonishing; good writers, are so to speak mediumistic to the deeper stirrings of life of their time while they are still unknown to, or at any rate unsuspected by the public, politicians and current received opinion."[3] Chaman Nahal may be said to be one of such "good writers" who is mediumistic to the deeper stirrings of life of the Gandhian age. His magnum opus, *The Gandhi Quartet,* is a brilliant mirror of the Gandhian age which reflects "not merely the external features of the age but also its inner face, its nervous system, coursing of its blood and the unconscious promptings and conflicts which sway."[4]

Chaman Nahal emerges as a major figure among the Indian English novelists of the 1970s. All the same, he maintains that he belongs to the second generation of Indian English novelists. He says: "Though my own novels were published in the 70s and later, I consider myself as part of the second group of writers, by age and thematic involvements."[5]

A study of Nahal's fiction would reveal that he belongs to the humanistic tradition initiated by Anand in the thirties and carried on by Bhabani Bhattacharya and Kamala Markandaya in the fifties and the sixties. Nahal's themes include tradition versus Westernization, wife-husband relationship, internationalism, East-West encounter, satire on anglicized Indians, the three phases of India's epic struggle for freedom and vivisection of India into India and the Muslim Pakistan and the agony it caused to the millions of people on either side of the dividing border.

Chaman Nahal's first novel, *My True Faces* (1973) deals in main with the marital discord and the resultant conflict between Kamal and Malti. The conflict operates at several levels. Kamal's search for Malti finally becomes his quest for unravelling the mystery of life.

Azadi (1975), which won the Sahitya Akademi award for the year 1977, is one of the most comprehensive fictional accounts of the partition holocaust in Indian literature. Like Khushwant Singh's *Train to Pakistan* (1956), it shows how the partition of India held the subcontinent in a nightmare of horror and left a trail of phenomenal bitterness and misery.

The theme of *Into Another Dawn* (1977) is cosmopolitanism and international fraternity. In addition, there is the theme of the meeting of the East and the West at the level of human emotions. Nahal's next novel, *The English Queens* (1979) is a satire on the follies, affectations and moralities of the anglicized Indians. He goes on to "debunk the humbug of purely native India" as well.

The Crown and the Loincloth (1981) is a forceful recordation of the non-violent non-cooperation movement that swept the country during 1920-22. It is the story of the transmutation of the ordinary into the extra-ordinary by way of fusing the personal, the heroic and the wider national perspectives into an organic whole.

Nahal once again introduces the quest motif in his *Sunrise in Fiji* (1988). Harivansh Batra, the protagonist, is a successful and wealthy architect. He has built hundreds of homes for others, whereas his own remains unfinished. He realizes that modern civilizations based on Western notion of progress cater only to the body rather than to the soul. He is so disappointed that he believes he is going to commit suicide. Then he prays for health, money, good looks, intuitive knowledge and friendship. After his five prayers, he gives up the idea of dying. But just as he affirms his faith in life, he slips down among the boulders and dies.

The Salt of Life (1990) is a remarkable historical novel with a fine blend of fact and fiction, representing vast canvas of the Indian freedom struggle during 1930 and 1941. Dealing as it does with the epoch making Dandi March of Gandhi, it highlights the contribution made by such eminent men as Bhagat Singh and Subhas Chandra Bose to the freedom movement. It can also be approached as a novel of woman's emancipation in India of the 30s.

Soon after completing *The Salt of Life*, which is his second novel on the theme of Indian freedom struggle in the Gandhian age, Nahal started working on *The Triumph of the Tricolour* (1993) which deals with the third and final phase of Indian freedom struggle—Quit India movement. Though Gandhi is the central figure of the novel, the violent revolutionaries led by Jayaprakash Narayan play a significant role in liberating India from the shackles of the British rule.

The purpose behind writing *The Triumph of the Tricolour* was not only to cover the peak period of the freedom struggle but also to regroup the four novels—*The Crown and the Loincloth, The Salt of Life, The Triumph of the Tricolour* and *Azadi* into a quartet to be issued together as *The Gandhi Quartet*. As a result, *Azadi* which was written eighteen years ago, earlier than the other three novels, forms the last volume of *The Gandhi Quartet*. However, Nahal has to add an "Epilogue" to 1993 edition of *Azadi* in order to acquire a structural unity. Like the "Epilogue" in G.B. Shaw's *Saint Joan* and the "Knights' Apologia" in T.S. Eliot's *Murder in the Cathedral*, the "Epilogue" to *Azadi* rounds off the story of Indian freedom movement led by Gandhi and the partition of India by giving us a peep into the post-Independence political India.

II

By the end of the nineteenth century, there was a gradual decline in the euphoria generated by the achievement of Rammohun Roy, Vivekananda and other great leaders. Spiritual and social awareness was slowly giving place to political consciousness. During these years of transition and transformation, Gandhi was in South Africa, undergoing his apprenticeship. He finally returned to India in 1915. As Nehru observes in *The Discovery of India*: "And then Gandhi came. . . . He did not descend from the top; he seemed to emerge from the millions of India, speaking their language and incessantly drawing attention to them and their appalling condition . . . political freedom took new shape and acquired a new content." (361)

Starting his political career in India with the Champaran Movement in 1917, Gandhi struck immediate rapport with the masses, thinking with their minds, speaking their language, but so inexorably projecting his own ideology on to their minds as to transform their attitude to themselves and to their social ambience. His most singular achievement was pulling the masses out of the quagmire of ignorance, fear and apathy. He taught them the basic virtue of 'abhaya,' fearlessness. As Nehru points out: "The essence of his teaching was fearlessness and truth, and action allied to these, always keeping the welfare of the masses in view." (361) The emancipation of the masses from fear was the main achievement of the Champaran Movement and it was for this that the title of 'Mahatma' was spontaneously conferred on him by the masses.

Gandhi did not teach anything new. Seers and sages, from time immemorial, have been emphasizing certain eternal values and their observance in daily life. He only reiterated them. As he himself concedes: "I have nothing new to teach the people. Truth and non-violence are as old as the hills."[6] But the uniqueness of Gandhi's teaching was that he practised before he preached. This appealed to the masses and they unhesitatingly accepted whatever he taught and followed him, wherever he led. He led them ultimately to independence. This is precisely what sets Gandhi apart from other leaders of his day.

Till his death, Gandhi never wavered in his faith as a 'sanatanistic' Hindu. He had great reverence for the Hindu scriptures—the Vedas, the Upanishads and the *Bhagavadgita*. The eternal values of Hinduism like truth, 'dharma' and non-violence had great appeal for him. But he was never sectarian or dogmatic. He always maintained that no religion is infallible or perfect. Every religion had some element of truth in it. He observes: "After a long study and experience, I have come to the conclusion that (1) all religions are true, (2) all religions have some error in them, (3) all religions are almost as dear to me as one's own close relatives. My own veneration for other faiths is the same as that for my own faith."[7] It was, therefore, inevitable that he should ultimately go beyond all traditional concepts of religion and come to believe in a transcendental religion, the very basis of all religions. Answering a query of S. Radhakrishnan, Gandhi says: "I often describe my religion as the Religion of Truth, of late, instead of saying God is Truth, I have been saying Truth is God, in order more fully to define my religion. . . Nothing so completely describes my God as Truth."[8]

Gandhi's view of religion extended to every field of activity. Being a true 'Karma Yogi' (man of action), he did not look upon any human activity as being apart from religion. He maintains: "I do not know of any religion apart from human activity. It provides a moral basis to all other activities which otherwise they would lack, reducing life to a maze of 'sound and fury signifying nothing.'"[9] In other words, all human activity being directed to the goal of transforming man to a higher ethical and spiritual level, religion must necessarily coexist with politics. So Gandhi could never envisage any political activity devoid of a religious basis. For Gandhi, politics was meant to serve people. Only a man who recognizes the divinity that is in himself as well as in others and realizes that all are manifestations of that ultimate can have such a noble concept of politics.

Truth and non-violence were twin pillars of Gandhi's political creed. Explaining his concept of non-violence, Gandhi observes: "Complete non-violence is complete absence of ill-will against all that lives . . . (it) is therefore in its active form goodwill towards all life. It is pure love."[10] Non-violence involves conscious suffering and is an extremely active force. It has no place for cowardice or weakness. Gandhi always said that the votary of non-violence had to cultivate the capacity for sacrifice of the highest type which would free him from fear.

Satyagraha, the weapon forged by Gandhi, is born of truth and non-violence. He used it in his struggle against racism and imperialism. Radhakrishnan considers satyagraha and non-violence synonymous: "*Satyagraha,* or non-violence, is not for

Gandhi a quiescent or negative attitude. It is positive and dynamic. It is not non-resistance or submission to evil. It is resistance to it through love. . . . *Satyagraha* is belief in the power of spirit, the power of truth, the power of love by which we can overcome evil through self-suffering and self-sacrifice."[11]

If satyagraha was a weapon fashioned to fight against the British empire and make the nation free, Gandhi's fasts were no less potent and always brought about the desired result. As a devout Hindu, Gandhi was no stranger to fasting. But it was given to him alone to shape this essentially religious practice into a political weapon as well as a means of spiritual self-purification. He always insisted that fast was an integral part of his creed of non-violence which purified both his opponent and himself. He observed: "A genuine fast cleanses body, mind and soul. It crucifies the flesh and to that extent sets the soul free."[12]

Gandhi's fasts, particularly those unto death, had a specific purpose such as putting down a communal riot or preventing obnoxious political measures like the Communal Award. Sometimes he also went on fast to atone for the moral lapses of his followers. Whatever the objective, his fasts were not only a clear measure of his spiritual eminence but also thoroughly efficacious as the rioting communities or the alien government fell in line with his wishes.

Political freedom for Gandhi was meant to free the nation from foreign rule and also from the social evils besetting it. So Gandhi waged a relentless battle against the latter. Foremost among the social evils was untouchability. He said: "Untouchability is repugnant to reason and to the instinct of mercy, pity or love. A religion that establishes the worship of the cow cannot possibly countenance or warrant a cruel and inhuman boycott of human beings."[13] He looked upon untouchability not only as a crime against man and God but also as a divisive force breaking up the Hindu society.

Equally repugnant to Gandhi was the caste system. However, he makes a clear distinction between caste system and 'varna dharma.' 'Varna,' according to Gandhi, is a division of society based on heredity and aptitude. It is no doubt determined by birth but can be retained only through observance of the necessary obligations. It does not carry with it any concept of superiority or inferiority. He observed: "All *varnas* are equal, for the community depends no less on one than on another. Today *varna* means gradations of high and low. It is a hideous travesty of the original."[14] In other words, he was against the divisive system of caste as it is today but held that a division of society into classes based on function was not only beneficial but necessary.

As Gandhi was aware that the present day caste system based on birth keeps a large section of people in poverty and ignorance, he evolved a system of education to help them in more ways than one. It was called 'Nai Talim' (New Education) or Basic Education or Wardha Scheme of Education. He always maintained that education, particularly at the primary and secondary levels should aim at the integrated and harmonious development of the personality of the pupils. He also maintained that character development should be the primary goal of education. This could be achieved only by the teacher who became an object lesson to his students. Gandhi also held that education should necessarily include craft-training which would make one economically self-sufficient. Thus, his 'Nai Talim' is naturalistic in its setting, idealistic in its aim and pragmatic in its implementation.

To one who abhorred social inequality born of caste system, inequality of sexes was equally odious. After an intense spiritual struggle which culminated in his vow of celibacy, he came to appreciate the true role of women in family and society. The forms of struggle he adopted—satyagraha, prohibition, boycott of foreign goods, development of cottage industries—necessitated the involvement of women in large numbers. Gandhi visualized women as equal partners at all levels of national life. Malavika Karlekar observes: "It is perhpas not a mere coincidence then that today, as the country is riven once again by a range of divisive forces, the strength of women's mobilisation is being acknowledged anew."[15]

Gandhi was fully aware that freedom would be meaningless to the millions of Indians unless it also meant economic independence. But Gandhi was no economist in the ordinary sense of the word. However, with his abundant commonsense, intensely pragmatic outlook and with his fingers on the pulse of the common people, he could formulate the most suitable economic ideology for the Indian masses. He advocated spinning and weaving because it provided work for the overwhelming part of rural population who were without any work for a good part of the year. He always held that whatever goods that could be produced by the villagers should not be allotted to urban industries. He preferred production of various goods by the masses to mass production in the factories. Gandhi was aware that production of goods was in direct proportion to man's wants. So he advocated a limiting of one's wants. He agreed with J.B. Kripalani who had said: "The possession of material goods beyond that [one's wants], instead of working for the freedom and the happiness of the individual, works for his enslavement and, often, for his unhappiness."[16]

Gandhian ideology is rooted in the eternal human values handed down to us over centuries such as truth, love, righteousness, non-violence and tolerance. They transcend space and time. These values have been taught and retaught by the Upanishads, the *Gita*, the Buddha and Christ. Gandhi only reiterated them. Gandhian ideology also accommodates a number of contemporary issues like untouchability, communal violence, rural poverty and the status of women in society. In all these things, Gandhi stressed that means are as important as ends.

Gandhi's achievement can best be described as titanic. As Natwar Singh observes:

> No Gandhi, no freedom movement. It is as stark as that. No Gandhi, no miraculous generation of leaders like Motilal Nehru, C.R. Das, Vallabhbhai Patel, C. Rajagopalachari, Sarojini Naidu, Rajendra Prasad, Maulana Azad, Abdul Ghaffar Khan, Jawaharlal Nehru. One who could draw such men to him was no mortal. He was a repository of spiritual values. He civilised our political manners and humanised our conduct.[17]

III

Indian writing in English like all other new literatures of the world in English has been the outcome of national ferment and upsurge, which manifested itself as much in the socio-political life of the country. Creative writers like Romesh Chander Dutt, Bankim Chandra and Sri Aurobindo of the earlier times and K.S. Venkataramani, Bharathi Sarabhai, Mulk Raj Anand and Raja Rao of the more recent years were themselves champions of the nationalist cause and spokesmen of the national culture. As K.S. Ramamurti observes: "Political urgency, reformistic motivation, journalistic impulse and creative imagination seem to have criss-crossed in the speeches and writings of the leaders like Surendranath Banerjee, Gopalakrishna Gokhale, V.S. Srinivasa Sastry, Sarojini Naidu and Jawaharlal Nehru and created patterns of writings which carry with them an unmistakable literary quality."[18] Gandhi, who belongs to this class of personalities, has made a powerful impact on Indian thought, in general, and on Indian literatures, in particular.

Indian English novels like Toru Dutt's *Bianca* or *The Young Spanish Maiden* (1878) and R.C.Dutt's *Lake of Palms* (1902); *The Slave Girl of Agra* (1903) and Rabindranath Tagore's *Home and the World* (1919) and *The Wreck* (1921) were written before the 1930s. But, while *Bianca* is incomplete, Tagore's novels are translations from Bengali. So there was no school of Indian English fiction proper before the 1930s. As Makarand R. Paranjape says: "the early novelists used their works to promote social reform. They espoused several liberal causes, campaigning for the education of women, the upliftment of depressed classes, widow-remarriage, and against child-marriage, dowry, superstition, *sati*, and untouchability, to list a few examples."[19] However, as M.K. Naik says, "there came a sudden flowering of Indian fiction in English in the 1930s—a period during which the star of Gandhiji attained its meridian on the Indian horizon. Under the leadership of Gandhiji, the Indian freedom-struggle, already more than a generation old, became so thoroughly democratized that the freedom-consciousness percolated, for the first time to the very grass-roots of Indian society and revitalized it to the core. It is possible to see a close connection between this development and the rise of the Indian novel in English."[20] Incidentally it was the period in which Gandhiji became almost a household name. Naturally, the Indian English novelists were bound to give creative expression to the new political and social aspirations of the people. Mulk Raj Anand and Raja Rao who started writing during the 1930s convincingly demonstrate the impact of Gandhi on the Indian masses in their novels. Apart from these two, K.S. Venkataramani, R.K. Narayan, Nayantara Sahgal, Kamala Markandaya and Manohar Malgonkar have all written novels on the freedom struggle.

The events that followed independence have figured in the novels of Khushwant Singh, Anita Desai and Salman Rushdie. Makarand R. Paranjape observes: "The dominant ideology of several of these novels on the freedom struggle may be characterized as nationalistic. Of course, nationalism rarely reached a revolutionary dimension except in the works of those who wrote at the height of the freedom movement or who were themselves involved in it. With the rest, it became a comfortable majority position that they could easily adopt in retrospect of its obvious success—an attitude shared by most of us today. In other words, the Indian English novel remained bourgeois, albeit liberal." (214)

Gandhi is introduced into the Indian English fiction in various ways. He appears as a character in Mulk Raj Anand's *Untouchable* (1935), *The Sword and the Sickle* (1942) and *Little Plays of Mahatma Gandhi* (1991), K.A. Abbas's *Inqilab* (1955), R.K. Narayan's *Waiting for the Mahatma* (1955) and Nagarajan's *Chronicles of Kedaram* (1961). Though he does not appear as a character in K.S. Venkataramani's *Murugan, the Tiller* (1927) and *Kandan, the Patriot* (1932) or Raja Rao's *Kanthapura* (1938), Gandhi is the driving force and is represented by idealized characters. Gandhi's followers appear in Bhabani Bhattacharya's *So Many Hungers!* (1947), Mrs. Sahgal's *A Time to be Happy* (1957) and R.K. Narayan's *The Vendor of Sweets* (1967).

In the twenties and early thirties, Gandhi was not the undisputed leader of the masses. There were many who did not have faith in his non-violent non-cooperation movement. But his social reforms like eradication of untouchability, and picketing toddy shops and sarvodaya ideals received the attention of one and all. The humiliated and long neglected section of the society at last found one who championed their cause. Many Indian English novelists like K.S. Venkataramani and Mulk Raj Anand felt that Gandhi was more effective as a social reformer. This is clearly revealed in their *Murugan, the Tiller, Kandan, the Patriot*, and *Untouchable* respectively.

By the late thirties and forties, Gandhi with his successful Salt Satyagrahha proved to the world the effectiveness of non-violent struggle for independence. Apart from his ahimsa, his love of truth and spirit of sacrifice made him the guiding spirit of the Indian freedom struggle. Influenced by him, many sacrificed what little they had for the sake of making India a free country. This is best illustrated by characters like Devesh Basu in Bhabani Bhattacharya's *So Many Hungers!* and the young Raja Raman in Manjeri Isvaran's "Between Two Flags." K.S. Venkataramani believes that economic reforms must be based on the revival of village life. Murugan, Ramachandran and Kethari are the three important characters in the novel. All of them belong to the village of Alavandi. Kethari becomes a lawyer, Ramachandran with all his love for village life is forced to work in a provincial town. Before leaving Alavandi, he has to sell the lands he inherited from his ancestors. Murugan the honest tiller, under the influence of one Thoppai, opens a toddy shop. By the time they come together again after a long time, they realize that one can lead a contented life by tilling one's three acres of land. Sarvodaya ideals are always in the background but in the climax "they actually become the hero." As Ramaswami describes, *Murugan, the Tiller* is "a novel of Gandhian ideals."

K.S.Venkataramani dedicates *Kandan, the Patriot* to "the unknown volunteers in India's fight for freedom." Kandan is an Oxford graduate and gains entry into the I.C.S. But he gives up his glittering post and decides to do some "public work" which includes working for political freedom, social emancipation and progress. Though Gandhi himself does not figure in the novel, he "dominates by proxy. It is his ideals and aspirations that the heroes of the novel are implementing. Kandan is a patriot as well as a social reformer."[21] Kandan joins the nationalists who are offering satyagraha at Tarangambadi. He dies when the police open fire to disperse the satyagrahis.

While Venkataramani is attracted by Gandhi's Sarvodaya ideal, Gandhi's love for the outcastes and his efforts to eradicate untouchability draw Anand to Gandhi. Anand visited Sabarmati to show the script of his novel 'Bakha' to Gandhi and draw inspiration and strength from him. Anand was impressed by Gandhi's sincerity, love of truth and love for the downtrodden. Anand admits: "the warmth towards Bakha, which has made this character lovable to many people, may, to some extent, have emerged from my warmth towards the person of Gandhi."[22]

Anand introduces Gandhi as a character in *Untouchable.* Anand is objective in his portrayal of Gandhi. He makes the innocent victim, Bakha, listen to every word of Gandhi in rapt attention, with the hope that his misery and humiliation would come to an end. But Gandhi offers no immediate solution. Instead, it is the machine-flush system, that raises some hope of relief in Bakha, the untouchable. In *The Sword and the Sickle,* Anand shows how Lalu, the protagonist, though impressed by Gandhi's peasant-like appearance and sincerity, refuses to be convinced of the effectiveness of Gandhi's non-violent struggle. Both in *Untouchable* and *The Sword and the Sickle*, Anand questions the effectiveness of Gandhian solution to the problems of untouchables and the peasants.

Unlike Mulk Raj Anand, Raja Rao does not present Gandhi as a character in *Kanthapura*. Nevertheless, he gives a vivid and faithful account of the impact of Gandhi on rural India. The image of Gandhi as presented by Raja Rao is an exemplary image because to him Gandhi is an avatar of Vishnu. To many people in Kanthapura, Gandhi is the invisible God and Moorthy is the visible avatar. Moorthy's efforts to eradicate untouchability and make the villagers spin, weave and wear hand-spun cloth meet with some resistance. As C.D. Narasimhaiah points out: "For throughout the novel idealization is accompanied by constant disapprovals of 'this Gandhi business' and 'Gandhi vagabondage,' the cynicism of friends, and hostilities—veiled and open—from neighbours."[23] But Moorthy slowly succeeds in making the freedom struggle take roots in Kanthapura. As the oppressive government uses brute force against the villagers, some of them die and others leave Kanthapura and settle in a new village. Moorthy is drawn towards the Congress activities led by Jawaharlal Nehru. Though Kanthapura is destroyed in the physical sense of the word by the imperialist government, the spirit of the villagers remains undaunted. They believe, "He will bring us Swaraj, the Mahatma. And we shall be happy."[24]

As in *Kanthapura*, in *The Cow of the Barricades* (1947) also, Raja Rao deals with the fight for India's freedom and Gandhi's impact on people. Gandhi, as in *Kanthapura*, is in the background. On the advice of the Master, the apostle of peace, people stop buying foreign cloth, stop serving the red-men's government and refuse to pay taxes. The workmen build barricades to prevent the army from entering the city. But the Master says: "No barricades in the name of the Mahatma, for much blood will be spilt. No, there shall be no battle, brothers."[25]

The tense situation appears to make Gauri the cow, the central figure of the short story, sad. Somebody even sees "a tear, clear as a drop of Ganges" running down her cheeks. When the city is about to be assaulted by the red-men's army, Gauri climbs the top of the barricades. The crowd, the workmen begin to chant *Vande Mataram.* Soon, the red-men's army joins the crowd and all of them begin to shout "Victory to the Mahatma! Mahatma Gandhi ki jai!" Angered at this, the chief of the army fires a shot and kills Gauri. Then, peace comes back to the people. Gauri symbolizes Mother India. Gandhi always wanted India to be a land of peace with unwavering faith in ahimsa and love every one like a mother with infinite compassion. Raja Rao makes Gauri

> Verily the Mother, herself,
> Bharat Mata, Mother India.[26]

Like Raja Rao, Bhabani Bhattacharya in his novel *So Many*

Hungers! presents the impact of Gandhi on people through the idealized character, Devesh Basu: "A truly Gandhian character—in precept as well as in practice—Devesh Basu stands for love, truth, and non-violence."[27] He is called Devata by the villagers. Though more than seventy, he is energetic and always inspired by Gandhian ideology. He runs a school for the villagers. He says: "Mass literacy is a danger for the rulers. It would, they know, make the trampled ones conscious of their birthright—the right to live as human beings."[28] Devata is non-violent both in thought and action. As with Gandhi, his love embraces all. He dislikes the British rule in India but not the British.

Devata is not only inspired but inspiring, Consequently, Rahoul, a budding professor and Kajoli, a peasant-girl join the liberation movement. After her village is destroyed by the police, Kajoli seeks shelter in Calcutta. As a result of the famine and man-made scarcity, she finds none coming forward to help her and her mother. Finally, she makes her grim decision. "She would sell the last thing she owned—herself." At this juncture, she hears the news that Devata is fasting unto death in the prison. Devata's advice asking the villagers not to betray the flag and themselves rings in her ears. Though "hunger-trapped," she decides to be "strong" and becomes a newspaper vendor. She is really "a living tricolour."

While the young Rahoul in Bhabani Bhattacharya's *So Many Hungers!* sacrifices his job for the sake of the country, the sixteen-year-old Raja Raman in Manjeri Isvaran's short story "Between Two Flags," sacrifices his future in response to Gandhi's call. Though Raja Raman is only sixteen, he loves India so much that he does not like the presence of the British in India. He refuses to salute the Union Jack at school. He is not deterred by the threatening words of the Headmaster. He has so much faith in Gandhi that he visualizes free India and tells his father: "I salute the flag of my country and the empire for which it stands, with many nations but all one and indivisible, with liberty and justice for all."[29] But his father, a loyal pillar of the alien government, thinks that what Gandhi and the Congress have been propagating is nothing but nonsense. He decides that his son must be put out of mischief's way. So he slaps his son. As a result, Raja Raman experiences a conflict of loyalties—loyalty to the Union Jack and loyalty to Gandhi. He thinks:

> It was an insult to our Motherland, an insult to our respect, to go on saluting the Union Jack when our patriots were being gagged and muzzled, beaten and thrown into goals by the whitemen. (85)

So he decides to leave his father, mother and sister and join the freedom struggle. But before he leaves his home, he breaks into pieces the portrait of King George V. He does not return home even after India gains independence. No one knows what the alien government did to him. Nobody knows whether he is alive or not: "But he remains as the deathless symbol of an independent spirit that has won, waving the banner of Free India, singing the song of ecstasy." (89)

The image of Gandhi as presented by Manjeri S. Isvaran is that of one who turns ordinary youngmen into 'a new type of warrior'—the soldiers of the non-violent army, who sacrifice their future for making India independent.

Thus, a study of the pre-Independence Indian English fiction dealing with Gandhi reveals certain facets of his image. K.S. Venkataramani presents Gandhi as an agrarian reformer with his sarvodaya ideal and as a nationalist with patriotic fervour. Mulk Raj Anand shows Gandhi as an ineffective social reformer with his programme of removal of untouchability and with his movement of non-violence. Raja Rao reveals the impact of Gandhi on Indian scene, showing how he produced thousands of little Gandhis and how he spread the message of peace throughout the country. Bhabani Bhattacharya and Manjeri S. Isvaran depict the tremendous influence that Gandhi exercised on a few individuals in India who translate into action what he stood for.

IV

A critical reader cannot but observe that R.K. Narayan, K.A.

Abbas and Nagarajan in a way, anticipate the course of events in post-Independence India. Gandhi had no illusions regarding his followers with the exception of a few like Jawaharlal Nehru and Patel. Most of the others have their own interests at heart. This is clearly brought out by the portrayal of Seth Maneklal Shah in *Inqilab* of Abbas, the Chairman and the timber-contractor in R.K. Narayan's *Waiting for the Mahatma*, Jagan in *The Vendor of Sweets* and Vanchi in Nagarajan's *Chronicles of Kedaram*. They are always ready to use Gandhism as a stepping stone for their upward climb to power and popularity. However, the majority of the characters, the average men and women, who form the silent, patient majority of society, are sincere in their loyalty to Gandhi and ideals. These are best illustrated by such characters as Anwar in *Inqilab* and Nirmala in *Chronicles of Kedaram*. Their faith never wavers and their loyalty is never shaken.

In *Inqilab*, K.A. Abbas presents Gandhi as a votary of Hindu-Muslim unity with his unflinching faith in the oneness of religion and as an apostle of non-violence. The protagonist, the young Anwar Ali's baptism into Gandhism takes place at the highly impressionable age of eight. Every day, Anwar sits besides his father and listens to the elders talking about Rowlatt Bills, Martial Law, Hartal, Congress, Muslim League, Gandhi's satyagraha and ahimsa. Of them: "two things instinctively appealed to him—not to obey the unjust laws of the Government and not to kill any one."[30] He learns from his father the meaning of Swaraj. Thus, Anwar is influenced by Gandhi even before he meets him. He remembers what Gandhi repeatedly tells people about religion. Gandhi declares: "My Hindu instinct tells me that all religions are more or less true. All proceed from the same God, but all are imperfect because they have come down to us through imperfect human instrumentality."[31] Anwar is happy because people appear to have understood the importance of Gandhi's words: "These were exciting and memorable days! Seldom before had Hindus and Muslims fraternized so openly, so enthusiastically." (72) Anwar proudly tells his father: "I also like Mahatma Gandhi." (57)

Unlike Bakha in *Untouchable,* Lalu Singh in *The Sword and the Sickle* and Sriram in *Waiting for the Mahatma,* the young Anwar in *Inqilab* appears to have understood Gandhi well. So in the midst of the people who have forgotten camaraderie and bonhomie that have existed till yesterday, and who have now started killing each other in the name of religion, Gandhi remains the only peace-maker to Anwar. He decides to meet Gandhi in spite of his father's newly developed hatred of Hindus.

Gandhi greets Anwar with a smile and asks him to sit down. Anwar does not know how to convey his anguish to the Mahatma. He bursts into tears. Then

> The *Charkha* stopped creaking and the Mahatma without saying a word, moved towards the boy and put a hand over his head, taking off the fez cap and gently stroking Anwar's short hair. There is such tenderness in his touch that Anwar felt even more helpless and sobbed violently. 'Oh Mahatmaji,' he cried out between the sobs, 'please do something about these Hindu-Muslim riots. Please! Please! only you can save us all. (127-28)

After saying these words, he looks at Gandhi's face and feels relieved: "Now he knew why they called him Mahatma, a Great Soul. On his face was look of such suffering, kindness and pity, as if he personally felt the misery of every single human being." (128) Instead of "mocking" a whimpering boy, Gandhi gives him an understanding smile. The voice of God or the Inner Voice shows Gandhi the way and he undertakes fast for twenty-one days. The riots immediately stop.

The image of Gandhi as presented by Abbas is objective. He presents an estimate of Gandhi both by his admirers and by people who differ from him. Nehru disagrees with Gandhian theory of trusteeship. Some are angry with Gandhi for supporting the Railway labourers and they call Gandhi 'bania'—seller of flour and pulses. Even Anwar does not approve of certain actions of Gandhi. He wonders why Gandhi does not dissuade people from touching his feet or carry away the dust "sanctified by his bare feet": "Anwar found his earlier feeling of exultation considerably chilled by the religious aspect of the Mahatma's Satyagraha." (286) Perhaps, this is the view of Abbas also.

While Gandhi appears only in a few scenes in *Inqilab,* he appears more prominently in R.K. Narayan's *Waiting for the Mahatma.* Narayan's Gandhi loves truth and children, enforces discipline, lives with the untouchables, preaches non-violence, stays where people are suffering and inspires people to take part in the freedom movement. He sees an untouchable boy on the premises of the Municipal Chairman's spruced up 'bungalow.' He immediately goes to stay in the colony of untouchables. As S.C. Harrex observes: "Although many critics have found Narayan's portrait of Gandhi unconvincing, Gandhi does come alive in the above scene—particularly as a reformer interested in untouchables as individual persons, as a teacher who influences others by example."[32]

Gandhi once again comes alive when he refuses to attend the independence day celebrations. Instead, he goes to Calcutta where fresh riots break out because his "place was where people were suffering and not where they were celebrating." Followed by Bharati and others, Gandhi visits villages affected by communal riots. He consoles the victims of riots. He forbids everyone to refer to anyone in terms of religion as Muslims, Hindus or Sikhs. He pities the perpetrators of the crimes. He asks Bharati to take care of the children who have lost their parents in the riots. The children are given the names of flowers and birds and no one knows whether they are Muslim children or Hindu. Thus Narayan presents an exemplary image of Gandhi.

But Narayan's intention is to show Gandhi's impact on the average Indian and to present an ironic portrayal of the response of some persons to Gandhi's teachings. Sriram, the protagonist, does not know the difference between Subhas Bose and Gandhi. He becomes a follower of Gandhi so that he can be near Bharati, the foster daughter of Gandhi, whom he loves. He weaves, wears hand-spun cloth, reads the *Gita* and takes part in the Quit India movement in his own way. When India becomes a free country, he feels proud of himself because he has contributed his mite to the freedom struggle. The timber-contractor has

Gandhi's portrait in his house, donates five thousand rupees to the Harijan Fund. But he does not apply Gandhian ideology to daily life. As he is afraid of the authorities, he attends the loyalist meetings. The Municipal Chairman spends a lot of money in welcoming Gandhi. But he belongs to the group of people who want to raise their stock by staying close to the Mahatma.

If Sriram in *Waiting for the Mahatma* becomes a follower of Gandhi for the sake of the woman he loves, Jagan in *The Vendor of Sweets* becomes a follower of Gandhi because he ardently desires to be revered as a follower of Gandhi. Gandhi's speech at Malgudi explaining the real significance of human action and service inspires Jagan. As a result Jagan

> joined the movement for freeing India from foreign rule and gave up his studies, home and normal life and violated the British laws of the time. Neither the beatings from the police nor the successive periods of prison life ever touched him when he remembered that he was performing service.[33]

He goes on chanting the name of Bapu day in and day out and always tells others that every action of his is influenced by Gandhian principles. He spins every day for an hour and wears hand-spun cloth. He wears only "ahimsak chappals"—sandals made from the hide of animals that died a natural death.

However, Narayan soon reveals the true colours of Jagan: "His reminiscential mood slurring over the fact that he had failed several times in the B.A., ceased to attend the college and had begun to take his examination as a private candidate long before the cause of Gandhi." (33) He pulps the left-over sweets back and fries them afresh in a new shape. When he sees a hungry vagrant begging for a handful of rice, he thinks that vagrant is a disgrace to the nation because the latter is not begging for public cause. He hoodwinks the tax officials because "Gandhi had made no reference to the sales tax anywhere." Like Gandhi, he renounces everything, but not his cheque-book. Thus, Narayan, the comic novelist, presents the response of certain people to Gandhian ideology in his own characteristic ironical way.

Like R.K. Narayan, Nagarajan also presents an exemplary image of Gandhi in his *Chronicles of Kedaram*. Like Jagan in *The Vendor of Sweets*, Vanchi in *Chronicles of Kedaram* subverts Gandhian ideals to feather his own nest. But Nagarajan presents characters like Nirmala who adore Gandhi and adopt his teachings in their daily life to the last dot.

In *Chronicles of Kedaram,* Gandhi appears in just two scenes. He accepts the invitation of Vanchinatha Sastri, the president of the local Congress Committee and visits Kedaram. Then, he addresses the people and resolves the long-standing dispute between the two Iyengar sects. Nirmala, under the impact of Gandhi, begins to work for harijan welfare. Later, she gives away all her assets to be used for the uplift of Harijans and joins Gandhi in Sabarmati. Koni's father has a high regard for Gandhi: "Gandhi was a saintly man, that he was working for the people and, in doing so, even went to the length of opposing the Government."[34]

However, critics like K.R. Srinivasa Iyengar and N. Radhakrishnan are not happy about Nagarajan introducing Gandhi as a character in the novel. Srinivasa Iyengar says: "It is difficult to say whether Nagarajan is praising Gandhi or pulling somebody's legs. There are other ambivalent touches, too, and one feels that, on the whole, it would have been better had Nagarajan not introduced Gandhi overtly into the story."[35] N. Radhakrishnan points out: "Nirmala's decision to throw herself at the feet of the Mahatma brings out the charismatic personality of Gandhi and his influence on the Indians much better than what is revealed from his role as a mediator in a quarrel and as a vote-catcher."[36] These critics think so because the long standing feud between the two Iyengar sects which Gandhi resolves is not of any national importance. Vanchi on whose invitation Gandhi comes to Kedaram is selfish and addicted to cars and mistresses. He never acts out of altruistic motives. Once a loyalist, Vanchi knows which way the wind is blowing. He starts wearing khaddar and becomes a member of the Congress and succeeds in making Gandhi visit Kedaram. As the narrator says: "He [Vanchi] won. Gandhiji capitulated. . . . Vanchi had 'hooked the fish'. . . an irreverent phrase but apt." (178)

While Nagarajan presents Gandhi in his *Chronicles of Kedaram* as one who offers a healing touch to the feuding factions and at the same time like R.K.Narayan shows how pseudo-followers like Vanchi exploit him for their selfish ends, Mulk Raj Anand strives to present the multi-faceted personality of Gandhi in his *Little Plays of Mahatma Gandhi*. Gandhi appears as a character in *Untouchable*. He offers only a few words of solace to Bakha, the protagonist, who belongs to the suffering class. Anand once again introduces Gandhi as a character in *The Sword and the Sickle*. Neither Lal Singh, the protagonist, nor the revolutionary group which teaches him political lessons has much respect for Gandhian principles. Thus, in both *Untouchable* and *The Sword and the Sickle*, no immediate Gandhian solution is offered to the raging issues.

After nearly five decades of writing, Mulk Raj Anand once again introduces Gandhi as a character in *Little Plays of Mahatma Gandhi*. It is the first part of the work in progress—an epic novel, *And So He Plays His Part*. Always innovative and original, Anand breaks the conventional novel form and writes *Little Plays of Mahatma Gandhi* in dramatic dialogues. The novel is placed in the Sabarmati Ashram, where Krishan Chander Azad comes to show his first draft of "Bakha" in 1930. Gandhi tells Azad that if he wants to stay in the Ashram, he must take three vows: not to look at women with desire, not to drink liquor and to clean the latrines once a week, as they do by turns. To Azad's queries, Gandhi humorously but firmly replies that the former can dream of his girl friend at night and he can drink in London, but not in the Ashram.

Mahatma Gandhi is not a writer in the usual sense of the word. But his remarkable imaginative understanding of the creative process is revealed in his sound advice to Azad. Gandhi goes through the pages of the script of "Bakha." He tells Azad that Harijans never talk in big words. He exclaims if he wants "to make them into Dr. Johnsons!" Azad feels humbled. Gandhi advises him to say what the poor and Harijans say and "write of life as it really is." Azad realizes the importance of Gandhi's advice: "It's from him that KCA [alias Mulk Raj Anand] learns that a writer should never forsake integrity—that he must empathize with his characters to comprehend their inner being."[37]

Azad learns from Gandhi that the caste system was division of labour and "insofar as it connotes distinctions in status, is an evil." Gandhi chants Rama 'nama' and has immense faith in the efficacy of prayer. But he wants to shift people's mind from God to man so that they serve 'Daridranarayan.' Gandhi says that it is not religion but ritual that is the curse of mankind. Lack of genuine faith in one's own religion is the cause of communal clashes. Azad finds it difficult not to agree with Gandhi. Bapu practises ahimsa both in thought and action. But he does not make a blind fetish of ahimsa. Realizing that the injured calf in the ashram cannot recover and even groaning seems to pain her, Gandhi agrees to mercy killing.

As the crops fail, the peasants of Bottial village near Bardoli find it difficult to pay taxes. Then the police beat them, loot their houses and assault the women. Thinking that retaliation by the peasants would go against Gandhi's principle of non-violence, Vallabhbhai asks them not to resist the police. But Gandhi says:

> No Ahimsa before tigers! If the honour of women is outraged you die in their defence. . . . I have never preached cowardice! If people have misunderstood me, it is my fault. . . . Non-violence is soul force. We have to be strong enough inside us to decide what to do. It is cowardly to run away from danger.[38]

Azad, a witness to all this discovers a new Gandhi before him.

Gandhi declares that people must live by the sweat of their brow. Machines must produce those things which cannot be produced in the villages. Ordnance factories are not signs of progress. He rejects western economy but adds that the rich should become trustees. These words of Gandhi shake Azad's faith in Marxism. Even in the midst of hectic political activity, Gandhi retains his sense of humour and continues to think of the common man. It helps him remain his usual self even in a crisis. When everyone is waiting for his decision on the new campaign against continued British oppression, Gandhi invites Subhash

Bose to inaugurate the new temples—the latrines for slum dwellers. Later, he joins children in enjoying the tricks played by two monkeys and somersaults with the boys.

In *Little Plays of Mahatma Gandhi*, Anand has no intention of idealizing any of his characters, including Gandhi. So he frankly reveals the opinions expressed by others about Gandhi because the latter always welcomes criticism. For instance, he recalls what Rajendra Prasad said of Gandhi's failure. Gandhi "failed to convert even those Muslims who said they were nationalists—to your [Gandhi's] idea of national education. I mean the poet Iqbal!" (114) Anand reveals how many of the 'ashramites' including Kastruba, have not completely imbibed the teachings of Gandhi. When the eighty-year-old Murli loses control on his bowels while having a meal, everyone goes away. Even Kasturba turns her back on the scene. Then Gandhi and Azad help Murli.

While painting Gandhi's failures, Anand is not blind to the positive aspects of his ashram life. Gandhi says that the rewritten novel of Azad shows that the latter has understood the agony of the untouchable protagonist and told the truth. He asks Azad to go out with love and meet the people in the interior. Azad, who has refused to call Gandhi Bapu, now touches his feet and receives his blessings.

Anand also shows how Gandhi makes a strong impression on Azad by giving a talisman. Gandhi tells Azad that whenever he wants to do something he must "recall the face of the poorest and the most helpless man" and ask himself if it is going to be of any help to such underprivileged. He must also ask himself: "Will it lead to Swaraj or self rule for the hungry and also spiritually starved millions of our countrymen?" (136-37) This is in fact, Gandhi's advice as much to every Indian as to Azad.

Yet, critics may wonder whether Mulk Raj Anand presents Gandhi as a bundle of contradictions in *Little Plays of Mahatma Gandhi*. A close study of the novel reveals Gandhi as

> saint, politician, an intimate human being of the earth earthy, with his head raised to the sky. He is known to contain in himself a multitude of contradictions. He con-

> verts a drunkard into sobriety. He allies himself with the thief who accuses Capitalist Ambalal Sarabhai of being a bigger thief. He exhorts peasants to whom he has preached non-violence to answer back the police violently, if they molest their women.[39]

These apparent inconsistencies are clearly explained by Chandrashanker Shukla, who says that to Gandhi, the votary of truth, "consistency lies in living upto the truth as he sees it from moment to moment. . . . There can be, there ought to be no uniformity in the actions of a man whose life undergoes a continual growth and who goes on rising in the spiritual scale."[40]

Thus, a study of *Little Plays of Mahatma Gandhi* reveals that the passing of forty years has brought about a perceptible change in Anand's attitude to Gandhi. Anand presents Gandhi as a humanist "par excellence." He seems to agree that unless people develop character, become fearless and remain united, their struggle for independence would not succeed.

Thus, a study of the pre-Independence and the post-Independence Indian English fiction reveals that the principal Indian English novelists who were profoundly affected by Gandhi are K.S. Venkataramani, Mulk Raj Anand, Raja Rao, R.K. Narayan, Bhabani Bhattacharya, K.A. Abbas, Nagarajan and Chaman Nahal. Each of these novelists seeks to present Gandhi in his own characteristic way. If some novelists like Venkataramani, Raja Rao and Bhabani Bhattacharya prefer to delineate the impact of Gandhi's impassioned idealism, hope and optimism on certain individuals and on Indian social life at large, others like Mulk Raj Anand, R.K. Narayan, K.A. Abbas, Nagarajan and Chaman Nahal present Gandhi as a character in their fiction.

V

While Mulk Raj Anand presents a dialectical and Raja Rao an ideal image of Gandhi, Chaman Nahal presents a realistic image of Gandhi in his *Gandhi Quartet*. Nahal highlights Gandhi's humility, foresight, pragmatism, uncanny perception, regard for everyone, patience and forbearance. Gandhi's humility is the hallmark of his greatness. Whenever someone says that he wants to serve Gandhi, the latter corrects him saying that all of them should serve the country. They can serve the country best by serving the poor. Gandhi's humility makes him tell his admirers not to call him 'Mahatma,' the noble soul. He often tells them that he is only an 'alpatma.'

Nahal throws ample light on Gandhi's foresight. Gandhi knows that once the non-violent non-cooperation movement starts, he would be arrested and the Congress would be in need of another leader. So he thinks of his successors. However, this does not "smack of hubris!" He leaves out his sons as they would imitate him. Nahal also shows how Gandhi's political acumen is always matched by his pragmatism. Before starting the non-violent non-cooperation movement, he goes round the county addressing the people. He works out plans for Congress committees down to the level of each village. He announces the decision to boycott the visit of the Prince of Wales, a year before, thereby paving the way for the nascent non-cooperation movement to assume gigantic proportions.

Gandhi's uncanny perception is driven home to us when he, from among the thousands of people who throng to him because of his mass appeal, notices the true potential of persons like Jawaharlal. So he meets Motilal Nehru and requests him to allow his son to enter active politics. Nahal presents yet another facet of Gandhi's personality by describing how Gandhi reciprocates the faith people have in him by having affection and regard for everyone of them. He believes that there is something to be learnt from every other person. While marching to Dandi, his concern for the neglected and humiliated section of the society makes him drop the idea of going to the Himalayas on pilgrimage. Instead, he decides to go to places where people are being segregated and humiliated. Nahal also highlights Gandhi's capacity to remain unruffled and calm even in the midst of a stormy situation. When the whole nation is anxiously waiting for Gandhi's word on new course of action against the unwanted regime, Gandhi goes to see a bitch which is laying litter. He alone realizes that the ultimate remedy for their suffering at the hands of the alien government lies in enduring ceaseless suffering till India gains independence.

Chaman Nahal, the realist, does not simply idealize Gandhi. Nahal shows Gandhi's failure to judge people's inability to remain non-violent in the thick of the agitation. He also fails to make people realize the importance of handspun cloth and eradication of untouchability. Nahal also shows how many people including Kastruba and Jawaharlal Nehru fail to understand Gandhi and find him enigmatic. However, they have unshakable faith in Gandhi which continues to guide them, even after Gandhi's death.

NOTES

1. Jawaharlal Nehru, *The Discovery of India* (1946; Bombay: Asia, 1956), p. 361.
2. R.C. Majumdar, ed., *History and the Culture of the People* (Bombay: N.P., 1969), vol. 1, p. 368.
3. Walter Allen, *Reading a Novel*, pp. 18-19.
4. *Ibid.*
5. Chaman Nahal, *The New Literatures in English* (New Delhi: Allied, 1985), p. 89.
6. M.K. Gandhi, *Harijan*, 28 March 1936, p. 49.
7. *Sabarmati* (1928), p. 17.
8. Gandhi's words as quoted by Radhakrishnan and Muirhead, *Contemporary Indian Philosophy,* ed. Radhakrishnan and Muirhead (London: George Allen and Unwin, 1958), p. 21.
9. M.K. Gandhi, *Harijan* , 24 Dec. 1938, p. 393.
10. M.K. Gandhi, *Young India*, 9 March 1922, p. 141.
11. S. Radhakrishnan, "Mahatma Gandhi," *Basic Writings of S. Radhakrishnan,* ed. Robert A. Macdermot (Bombay: Jaico, 1987), p. 271.
12. M.K. Gandhi, *Young India,* 24 March 1920, p. 1.
13, M.K. Gandhi, *Young India,* 6 Oct. 1921, pp. 318-19.
14. M.K. Gandhi, *Harijan*, 28 Sept. 1934, pp. 261-62.
15. Malavika Karlekar, "The Relevance of Mohandas Karamchand Gandhi: A Contemporary Perspective," *Indian Journal of Gender Studies,* 2.1 (1995), p. 62.

16. J.B. Kripalani, *Gandhi: His Life and Thought* (1970; New Delhi: Govt. of India, Publications Division, 1991), p. 368.
17. K. Natwar Singh, "No Ordinary Mortal," rev. of *The Good Boatman: A Portrait of Gandhi* by Rajmohan Gandhi, *Frontline,* 3 Nov. 1995, p. 81.
18. K.S. Ramamurti, "Jawaharlal Nehru in Indian English Literature with Special Reference to the Novel," *Essays in Criticism on Indian Literature in English*, ed. M.S. Nagarajan et al (New Delhi: S. Chand, 1991), p. 52.
19. Makarand R. Paranjape, "Inside and Outside the Whale: Politics and the New Indian English Novel," *The New Indian English Novel,* ed. Viney Kirpal (New Delhi: Allied, 1990), p. 214.
20. M.K. Naik, "Gandhiji and Indian Writing in English," *Critical Essays on Indian Writing in English,* ed. M.K. Naik, S.K. Desai and G.S. Amur (1968; Madras: Macmillan, 1977), pp. 374-75.
21. N.S. Ramaswamy, *K.S. Venkataramani* (New Delhi: Sahitya Akademi, 1988), p. 53.
22. Mulk Raj Anand, "The Story of My Experiments with a White Lie," *Critical Essays on Indian Writing in English*, ed. Naik et al, p. 13.
23. C.D. Narasimhaiah, "Raja Rao's *Kanthapura*: An Analysis," *Critical Essays on Indian Writing in English,* ed. M.K. Naik et al, p. 251.
24. Raja Rao, *Kanthapura* (1938; Madras: Oxford University Press, 1984), p. 258
25. Raja Rao, "The Cow of the Barricades," *The Policeman and the Rose* (1947; New Delhi: Oxford University Press, 1978), pp. 38-39.
26. K.R. Srinivasa Iyengar, "Raja Rao," *Indian Writing in English* (1962; New Delhi: Sterling, 1990), p. 388.
27. G.S. Balarama Gupta, "Bhabani Bhattacharya's *So Many Hungers!*: A Study," *Aspects of Indian Writing in English*, ed. M.K. Naik (Madras: Macmillan, 1979), p. 213.
28 Bhabani Bhattacharya, *So Many Hungers!* (1947; Delhi: Orient Paperbacks, 1978), pp. 26-27.
29. Manjeri S. Isvaran, "Between Two Flags," *Stories from the East and the West,* ed. S. Ganapati (Madras: Emerald, 1983), p. 88.
30. K.A. Abbas, *Inqilab* (Bombay: Jaico, 1955), p. 8.
31. M.K. Gandhi, *Young India*, 29 May 1924, p. 180.
32. S.C. Harrex, "R.K. Narayan, Comedy of Manners and Arche-

types," *The Fire and the Offering* (Calcutta: Writers Workshop, 1978), vol. 2, p. 109.

33. R.K. Narayan *The Vendor of Sweets* (Mysore: Indian Thought Publications, 1967), p. 47.
34. K. Nagarajan, *Chronicles of Kedaram* (1961; Bombay: Asia, 1973), pp. 135-36.
35. K.R. Srinivasa Iyengar, "Gandhi Literature," *Indian Writing in English,* p. 288.
36. N. Radhakrishnan, "The Image of Gandhi," *Indo-Anglian Fiction: Major Trends and Themes* (Madras: Emerald, 1984), p. 78.
37. Shiv K. Kumar, "Gandhi on Stage: *Little Plays of Mahatma Gandhi,*" *The Novels of Mulk Raj Anand,* ed. R.K. Dhawan (New Delhi: Prestige, 1992), p. 226.
38. Mulk Raj Anand, *Little Plays of Mahatma Gandhi* (New Delhi: Arnold, 1991), p. 58.
39. "Front Flap," *Little Plays of Mahatma Gandhi.*
40. Chandrashanker Shukla, *Gandhi's View of Life* (Bombay: Bharatiya Vidya Bhavan, 1936), p. 10.

The Lion in the Loincloth: *The Crown and the Loincloth*

Chaman Nahal's *The Crown and the Loincloth,* which forms the first volume of *The Gandhi Quartet,* deals with India's struggle for freedom during 1915-1922. It recapitulates the first of the three phases of the Gandhian age, namely, the non-violent non-cooperation movement. It gives us a graphic picture of Gandhi's return to India in 1915, his extensive tour of India, the impact of Gandhi and his writings on people, and his success in making the people protest against the Rowlatt Bills by boycotting the visit of the Prince of Wales. It also shows how Gandhi succeeds in making the women play a more active role in the liberation movement and in making the people realize the importance of spinning and weaving in achieving self-sufficiency at least in clothing.

Nahal begins the novel with an account of Gandhi's return journey to India in 1915 after his South African "Experiments with Truth" by the ship, *S.S. Arabia.* For one year he goes round the country meeting people. He teaches them the importance of the non-violent struggle against the British rule in India through his speeches and writings in *Young India* and *Navajivan.* When the imperialist government passes the heinous Rowlatt Bills, he asks the people to observe hartal and fast for one day and thereby register their protest against the Rowlatt Bills. Sunil, son of Thakur Shanti Nath, living at Ajitha, a small village in Punjab, is influenced by Gandhi's creed of non-violence and takes part in the hartal. Later, on Gandhi's advice, he makes the villagers take interest in spinning and weaving. Joined by Rehna, he opens khadi stores. After the butchery at Jallianwala Bagh, he goes to Simla Hills to redress the grievances of the plantation workers. Moved by the sad plight of the untouchables, he decides to work for their uplift and not to think of freedom struggle. After Rehna's death at Naini Tal, he goes to Lahore to see Shyama, his sister, and her husband, Rakesh, a member of the Himmat, a revolutionary outfit. While the whole nation is busy boycotting the visit of the Prince of Wales and observing non-violent non-cooperation movement, Rakesh and Charulata get ready to assassinate the Prince. But, Sunil thwarts their attempts, saves the Prince but dies in the process.

Nahal divides the novel into three parts—"Love," "Perspectives," and "Affirmation." In the first part, he describes Gandhi's love for motherland that is reeling under the alien rule and love of "the masses . . . the weak and the low. In the interest of the meek—the meek who filled the earth." [1] Nahal also describes love between Shyama and Rakesh and love between the married Sunil and Rehna and Kenneth Ashby's love of India and Indians.

In the second part, Nahal provides different perspectives of various characters on the freedom, non-violence, terrorist activities and love and their clash. Sunil's perspective on freedom undergoes a sea change after his stint with the plantation workers. While Rehna becomes an active khadi saleswoman and satyagrahi under the influence of Gandhi, her husband, Muzaffar grows critical of Gandhi and alleges that the character of the Congress is becoming increasingly Hindu. Rakesh, who does not believe in the efficacy of Gandhi's non-violent movement declares:

> And there can be no revolution except through the barrel of a gun. . . . Those in the higher echelons would never willingly surrender or give up their rule until they are dethroned, until they are pushed out. There will have to be a blood bath. (202)

While the married Sunil firmly believes that consummated love alone is love, Rehna tells him: "But I truly love . . . it is a very precious emotion and the only way to keep it alive is by not coming too close physically. Consummated love is no better than an affair." (291) Celia Ashby, Kenneth Ashby's American aunt, is objective in her view of Indian freedom movement and the violent and non-violent methods adopted to achieve it.

In the third part, as a result of the change brought about by time in him, Sunil is bent on making an affirmation. He dies while trying to save the Prince of Wales, the figure-head of the repressive government. After his death, Kusum, his wife, makes a similar affirmation. She, with her son, Vikram, joins Gandhi at Sabarmati: "And there seemed a lure in the thought of joining the ashram, a departure from the old, a taking on of the new and the unknown, that real affirmation implied." (453) She declares that hereafter her only duty will be to work for the lowly. In spite of calling off the first mass movement because of the violent incidents at a few places, Gandhi reaffirms his faith in non-violent non-cooperation with the government: "No, the irreducible demands would remain the same if his people wanted him to lead them. Non-violent non-cooperation with the government, and on *his* terms. No, he couldn't reduce himself further." (407)

Nahal introduces a few episodes with the specific purpose of throwing light on situations and character of Gandhi. In the first part, the episode of apparitions shows Gandhi making a retrospective evaluation of his "South African experiments of satyagraha," and concluding:

> Moral right was the only answer to moral wrong. Satyagraha was the term he coined for it—truth-force. And he was soon going to test it on a much wider scale. . . . Now he had the whole of India to play his role in. Much bigger issues were involved, much bigger forces; it also involved a bigger effort on his part. (38)

The episode of the heifer, Bhuri, reveals how the young Shyama could not suppress her desires and as a result eloped with Rakesh. The episode of Jawaharlal Nehru's birth and entry into active politics reveals Motilal Nehru's affection for his son and Gandhi's uncanny perception and persuasive skill. Gandhi perceives Jawaharlal's ability to successfully lead the nation. He succeeds in convincing Motilal Nehru that Jawaharlal's personality can find fullest expression only in political life.

The ordered and organized sequence of events and actions in *The Crown and the Loincloth* reveals Nahal's skill in constructing a well-knit plot. The plot is concerned with Gandhi's return to India from South Africa in 1915 on Gokhale's advice, his travels around the country, his call to the people to protest against the Rowlatt Bills through hartal and fast, the tremendous response Gandhi's call generates, his efforts to make the rural India become self-sufficient, at least in clothing, by spinning and weaving, his attempts to eradicate social evils like untouchability, the nationwide boycott of the visit of the Prince of Wales under his leadership and Gandhi calling off the non-cooperation movement, the first of the three phases of India's struggle for freedom after violence at Chauri Chaura.

The plot is also concerned with Gandhi succeeding in making Motilal Nehru allow his son, Jawaharlal, to enter active politics and Sunil, a follower of Gandhi, sacrificing his life while trying to save the life of the Prince of Wales at the hands of Rakesh, a revolutionary.

The Crown and the Loincloth is essentially a novel of character. Nahal's focus is more on delineation of characters in dealing with situations than on description of incident. While portraying his characters convincingly, Nahal takes every care to see that no character, however great and noble, is deified. Almost all the characters created by Nahal are round characters and as Forster says are "ready for extended life." "They are so well-realized that we can almost imagine them living in the world beyond the book."[2] Describing Gandhi's greatness, M.K. Naik says: "The glory that was Gandhi has left a permanent impress upon many aspects of modern India. Gandhiji's greatness was an unusual greatness in the sense that some men are great at small things; some others are great at one great thing; but Gandhiji belonged to that giant race of great men who are great at a great many things and whose greatness embraces large areas of human experience."[3]

Small wonder, therefore, if many Indian English novelists

like Raja Rao have presented the ideal image of Gandhi. But Chaman Nahal is aware of the fact that "Gandhi did not transform stone into bread, or grass into a charmed weapon to kill demons with. . . . He did not indulge in miracles. Yet millions after millions were thrilled by the sight of this man."[4] So he presents the realistic image of Gandhi in *The Crown and the Loincloth*.

Nahal begins the novel with what the critics of Gandhi think of him. Ba is unhappy because Gandhi has been torturing himself with too many vows. The apparitions of the two girls reveal how Gandhi punished them for no fault of theirs. The apparition of Harilal, his eldest son, calls him a monster for neglecting him. The apparition of Lakshmidas, his elder brother, accuses that Gandhi is an ungrateful fellow.

Lest the critics fail to understand Gandhi properly, Nahal gives a fairly elaborate account of the people who appreciated what Gandhi stood for in South Africa. The apparition of Kallenbach tells him that he has come out of faith in him. Mir Alam's apparition tells Gandhi that the latter's forgiveness has made him his follower. The apparition of Valliamma reveals the spirit of sacrifice that Gandhi inspires even in a sixteen-year-old girl.

Despite Gandhi's strong desire to serve the nation and not to lead people; he becomes the undisputed leader of the masses. But before deciding to lead the national movement for freedom, he wants to purify himself further so that he can remain unruffled, unmoved by pain and pleasure. He knows that the British government would adopt repressive measures. But he is not spineless:

> They may beat the life out of him but they couldn't bend him. He would actually touch the feet of the lowliest, as before God they were all equal; no one was high, no one low. But when they came and slapped him across his face or tried to crush him otherwise, they achieved nothing. His spine remained erect and firm. (29)

Gandhi as a leader is unique in more ways than one. For him

little things matter very much. He does not believe in long term plans for achieving anything or for solving problems. The promulgation of the heinous Rowlatt Bills provides him the right opportunity to wake up the consciousness of the millions of people living in villages and make them take part in the movement. No other leader before him has thought of this.

Nahal presents Gandhi not only as a great leader but also as an influential writer: "No one who has used the stuff of words on a massive scale has been as passionately purposive as Gandhi."[5] Sunil reads Gandhi's *Hind Swaraj* (*Indian Home Rule*) which the latter has written in 1908. It contains nearly a hundred pages. In it Gandhi repudiates Western civilization for all humanity. He says that love alone has power over evil. Evil must be resisted but with personal suffering, self-sacrifice and soul-force. After reading *Hind Swaraj*, Sunil realizes that non-violence is a greater force and power than violence. Under the influence of Gandhi's writings, he sacrifices his life, while trying to save the Prince of Wales, who represents the oppressive regime.

Gandhi, the satyagrahi, receives no less attention in the novel. After Dyer "had killed Gandhi's faith in the Englishman," Gandhi realizes that appeals, oral or written, to the government have ceased to be effective. He must invent "a new system of fighting them." But it has to be non-violent. He declares: "for I have now come to believe that the power of non-violence lies in its ability to work even in the midst of conflagration."[6]

Gandhi's invaluable gift to the people in various parts of the world who have been facing repression of some kind or other is satyagraha. Until now no one has come out with a better non-violent way of protest. J.B. Kripalani observes: "Every unbiased observer will admit that the method of satyagraha is a definite improvement upon the method of constitutional agitation of petition, prayer, and protest that marked the Congress politics before the advent of Gandhi."[7]

The Muslims, Sikhs and Hindus become one and take part in the satyagraha. The outside world becomes conscious of a face of India that the British has never told about "a face that they themselves had in all probability never known."

The novelist highlights what J.B. Kripalani calls Gandhi's "double programme, one for active and revolutionary periods when the tempo of political life is on the rise and the other for comparatively peaceful times." (179) The far reaching significance of Gandhi's double programme can hardly be exaggerated. The first type of programme, meant to be used during turbulent times, comprises dharna, protest, non-cooperation and satyagraha. The second type of Gandhi's programme, meant for peaceful times, consists of such social and economic activities as spinning, weaving, eradication of untouchability and the uplift of the poor and downtrodden.

Gandhi's mass appeal and charisma make the British anxious. They decide to counter it by inviting the Prince of Wales to India. But they know for sure that almost all Indians would be boycotting the visit of the Prince because of the boycott call given by Gandhi in 1920. So they arrest all the top leaders in the hope that the leaderless masses would not respond to the boycott call. Belying their hope, people in thousands come into the streets and greet the Prince with black flags and with shouts of 'Go back home.' Thousands of people throng to Gandhi. With his unfailing perception, he notices the true potential of persons like Jawaharlal. So he meets Motilal Nehru and persuades him to allow his son to jump into active politics. Jawaharlal Nehru is Gandhi's valuable gift to India.

Gandhi fails to judge people's inability to remain non-violent in the thick of the struggle. He is sad to hear the news about people everywhere indulging in violence. He himself is a witness to the anarchy in Bombay. The demonstrations against the visit of the Prince uplift his heart but the violence that follows disturbs him. So he calls off the movement. Many including Jawaharlal fail to understand the reason behind it and are angry with him: "The task of effectively training very large numbers in a very short time proved, however, too great and, rather than see his movement degenerate into civil war, Gandhi suspended the activities of his non-violent army."[8]

Many fail to realize the importance of Gandhi's call to wear handspun cloth and eradication of untouchability. The economic stranglehold of the British on India can be broken by boycotting the British-made goods. Then an alternative is found in khadi. Untouchability is discrimination against a section of our own people. In spite of Gandhi's appeal, many do not wear handspun cloth and continue to practise untouchability. This pains Gandhi. Thus, Nahal clearly shows Gandhi as a disappointed person.

Another facet of Gandhi's personality highlighted by Nahal is Gandhi's ability not to be angry with anyone. When he realizes that he is not properly understood by many people, Gandhi blames himself. He decides to purify himself further. He takes two more vows. He will wear loincloth and remain bareheaded. Reluctantly, he agrees to wear a shawl around him when it is cold:

> It is in the possession of the virtue of detachment from self that, I suggest, lies the source of Gandhi's authority. . . . The detached man has power, over his body because having effected its separation from the true self, he is enabled to use it as an instrument for the purpose of the self. That it is no accident that Gandhi can sleep at will at a moment's notice for any period that he likes to prescribe, no accident that he can deliberately lose or gain weight without altering his diet.[9]

Nahal clearly states that even if one understands Gandhi clearly, it is almost impossible to be a true Gandhian:

> One can only hope to be a partial one. . . . Gandhiji is freak. He is too honest, too bold, too daring, too resolute, too defiant, too fearless, too indomitable, too astute, too quick, too intelligent, too truthful. Only a freak can have these qualities in such extreme, and none of us can match him. We can only hope to go somewhere near him. (283)

In spite of the fact that only a few understand his ideology clearly, Gandhi's faith in people and the ultimate success of the non-violent non-cooperation movement remains firm. He declares that his

> irreducible demands would remain the same if his people wanted him to lead them. Non-violent, non-cooperation with the government, and on *his* terms. No, he couldn't reduce himself further; his people would have to raise themselves to his level. If any thing, he would make the non-violent, non-cooperation even more stringent. (407-8)

Gandhi is happy because now the Congress is a body of the masses. Its rural membership is twice the urban membership and it has smashed the British hold on the peasantry.

Of all the leaders, Gandhi alone succeeds in diagnosing the true reason for the violence that erupted during the boycott of the visit of the Prince of Wales. It is fear that has turned people violent. So his immediate task is to make people fearless. They should stop being afraid of authority before the next mass movement is launched: "Gandhi's simple injunction 'Be not afraid!' is his greatest gift to the Indian people. It is the act of ordinary citizens freeing themselves from fear of power and authority that heralds the dawn of a truly democratic era."[10]

While Gandhi is getting ready to make the people fearless and the next movement free of violence, he is arrested and sentenced to six years' imprisonment. However, Nahal asserts that the ultimate victory would be Gandhi's:

> Gandhi was arrested on charges of sedition. A week later, on March eighteen, 1922, a British judge sentenced Gandhi to six years' imprisonment on those charges. For the time being, the lion in the loincloth was caged. (466)

Chaman Nahal does not simply idealize Gandhi. In spite of his vow of celibacy, Gandhi cannot help looking at Kasturbai with desire. The abuses hurled at him for calling off the movement after Chauri Chaura incident make him think of committing suicide. Here he is impulsive. A leader of his stature should never be impulsive. But he admits these lapses and observes a fast as atonement. Herein lies his greatness.

Chaman Nahal frankly tells us what Gandhi's political critics and opponents think of him. Dyer, who is cast in the role of villain, calls Gandhi "crooked" and "seditious." He thinks that non-violence is a farce. Believing that love between the Muslims and the Hindus is impossible, he makes fun of the Khilafat movement. Seeing Gandhi everywhere in the role of a trouble-shooter, Dyer calls him "scheming." Gandhi's call for "a nation-wide hartal, a nation-wide strike" is only a "new drama" to Dyer. Had the government allowed Gandhi to proceed to the Punjab, he "would have finished him off with his own hands." How shallow Dyer is in his thinking when compared with Gandhi!

Nahal's portrayal of Motilal Nehru throws light on the role of the Moderates in India's struggle for freedom, Motilal's anxiety to father a son, his regard for Gandhi and the latter's impact on him. As a Moderate, Motilal declares that they are not at war against the British. While Gandhi believes in non-violent non-cooperation with the government to make the British quit India, Motilal believes in "asking for a gradual change, through parliamentary means, not through revolution." (355)

For Motilal, "to bring up five nephews and not a son of his own," aggravates his desire to have a son. When, at last his wife, Swarup Rani, presents him with a son, Motilal gives the name Jawaharlal, the jewel of jewels, to the boy. Though he was older than Gandhi by seven years, Motilal addresses Gandhi as Gandhiji. His love for Jawaharlal makes him request Gandhi to delay his son's "plunge into the political arena" till his son is "sure of himself." However, under the influence of Gandhi, he gives up his lucrative practice as a lawyer and becomes a member of the Congress Volunteers. He allows Jawaharlal also to discontinue his legal practice and become a full-time worker for the Congress. When they are arrested in 1921

> In the manner laid down by Gandhi, they offered no defence and took no part in the trials. Both were sentenced to six months' imprisonment. A fine was also imposed upon them which, again in the manner laid down by Gandhi, they refused to pay. (358)

While in jail, Motilal refuses to accept any favours from his friend, Sir Harcourt Butler, the Lieutenant-Governor. Like many others, Motilal also fails to understand the reasons that forced Gandhi to call off the non-violent non-cooperation movement.

The young Jawaharlal Nehru with "refined features and a shy, meditative smile" has a lot of affection and immense regard for his father. When in jail, he washes his father's clothes and prepares tea. As he finds "his father's argument convincing," Jawaharlal accepts his verdict in most matters. However, he is never afraid of his father. When he is asked to submit an account of all his expenses by his father, he refuses to do so. He asks his father whether the latter trusted him or not. Though studied in Harrow, symbol of the English establishment, he becomes a follower of Gandhi and gives up his legal practice. His regard for Gandhi makes him join the group of young men who pull the carriage with Gandhi in it, to Anand Bhawan. But he also fails to realize why Gandhi has called off the non-violent non-cooperation movement after violence at Chauri Chaura.

Nahal presents Kasturbai as Gandhi's bitter critic and as one who is eager to prove that she too can do what Gandhi does. Her strong desire is to be his equal by revealing that women also are brave enough to take part in the freedom struggle and go to jail. Gandhi understands that it is her way of telling him that he has neglected her all these years. In South Africa, after the death of Valliamma in 1913, she led the Indian women in their fight for their rights. "She disapproved of him on several counts." She considers him the most unpredictable and quite often she fails to "anticipate his moves." She always notices him to be restless and this baffles her most. She gives her consent to Gandhi's vow of celibacy. She is always eager "to serve him and please him."

Nahal's portrayal of Sunil brings to our mind Moorthy in Raja Rao's *Kanthapura*. Like Moorthy, Sunil is inspired by Gandhi's ideals and declares that the right approach to the problem the country is facing is a non-violent approach. He wants to serve Gandhi. But Gandhi corrects him by saying that he must serve India by becoming a khadi salesman. Later, Sunil goes to the Simla Hills to help the plantation workers. The miserable conditions in which they are living provide Sunil with a glimpse of real India. He understands that there are many things to be achieved immediately before independence. So he

> even withdrew the expression satyagraha from use—with which he had inflamed the labourers to fight the merchants. He could see that at least these hill people were not yet ready for any political fight. Their souls were buried in the earth under their soles, and they had to be resurrected before they could have a sense of the soul-force. If they could keep themselves clean, if they could earn their daily bread with dignity, if they could look upon each other with respect—those would be achievements enough for them. (264)

With the help of a local doctor, he becomes an itinerant medicine man. He will not ask the workers to fight for freedom because they are not ready for it. Similarly, after the Chauri Chaura incident, Gandhi realizes that his countrymen are not yet ready to fight for freedom through non-violence in its pristine purity.

Like Gandhi, Sunil is a social reformer. He is pained to see untouchability among the people in the Simla Hills. He decides to work for their uplift, a cause dear to Gandhi. On Gandhi's advice, he employs an untouchable boy, Chandru, as his servant. But soon he realizes how difficult it is to eradicate this obnoxious practice of untouchability. He is forced to send away Chandru. This disheartens Sunil. He feels frustrated and concludes:

> Liberty, independence, autonomy were as many words for them, a pastime of the rich or the privileged. They were not even roused by spiritualism. Since they prayed to the same gods as the Hindus, the gods apparently took sides, invariably letting them down; if Gandhi was another god, the caste Hindus could keep him. They would much rather continue to be slothful, slow and sluggish. (249)

Nahal makes his intention not to idealize the protagonist Sunil clear by describing at length the latter's role as a lover "cheated of the desired consummation" with Rehna and as a "sensualist" in his love for Priti. Rehna's strange lure makes Sunil neglect his wife, Kusum. He spends a passionate night, with Priti, the wife of a plantation worker. Finally, the adoration of the innocent plantation workers pricks his conscience. He opens his eyes to his wickedness and the lapse on his part. As soon as he leaves the Simla Hills, Priti fades away from his mind and life. Soon after Rehna's death, he is drawn to his wife. He sincerely asks Kusum for forgiveness. Now, he loves her and makes an affirmation to that extent time and again. Love becomes the guiding principle of his life. The same love makes him sacrifice his life while trying to save the Prince of Wales who represents the alien and oppressive government. Thus, Sunil makes a grand affirmation of love and non-violence that are so dear to Gandhi in his tragic death: "With sure instinct, again Nahal makes a rough sort of Gandhi-Sunil equation."[11]

Nahal presents Rakesh, a friend to Sunil, as a foil to him. Rakesh is "a nationalist—an Indian nationalist." He declares that he "won't rest until the last of the British are driven out of India." His conviction is that

> The entire Gandhian movement is misconceived; passive resistance will make an already feeble race even more feeble. You can't bring about revolution except through force, through show of strength. If the British are in India it is because of their power. And the movement to which I belong will counter power with power. (201)

Believing that "there can be no revolution except through the barrel of a gun," he becomes a terrorist.

There is ambivalence in the attitude of Rakesh and Shyama to each other. In spite of his hatred for landlords, he falls in love with Shyama, the daughter of Thakur Shanti Nath. He loves her. However, he loves more the cause for which he is prepared to die. Shyama loves him, but she has no faith in his creed of terrorism and political convictions.

Rakesh and other members of the revolutionary outfit, Himmat, plan to assassinate the Prince of Wales. But we are sure that such an act of violence would invariably fail within the framework of the novel. The attempt of Rakesh and his comrades to assassinate the Prince are foiled by Sunil. Sunil's sacrifice and the failure of Rakesh vindicate the victory of non-violence over violence.

While Sunil and Rakesh choose non-violent struggle and armed revolt respectively to gain independence, Thakur Shanti Nath prefers to wait and see. He represents the Moderates. He believes that one day the British would definitely quit India leaving Indians to rule themselves. So he is against embarrassing the government with "hartals, strikes, mass meetings, and jail going." His unshakable faith in the fair play of the British makes him conclude that the earthquake in which Rehna dies is only God's retribution to Indians for rebelling against the British. He finds fault with Bapu for launching the movement without giving proper training to the non-violent army. But the British government does not pay heed to the words of Moderates like Thakur Shanti Nath.

Among the women characters created by Nahal, Kusum stands foremost in the novel. As long as Sunil is alive, she lives for him in spite of his love for Rehna. After his noble death, Kusum's character acquires a new dimension. She makes her own affirmation by joining Gandhi at Sabarmati. She offers her little son as well to the nation: "and the grand affirmation of martyrdom by Sunil is matched, after his tragic death by Kusum's similar affirmation at Sabarmati, her dying to her old life and being reborn to the new, all her other duties fell away and only one remained, as Gandhiji had once said: towards the lowly!"[12]

Rehna is Nahal's unique creation. She is a blend of intellect, emotion, tragic fatality, and desire for death. Though she is married to Muzaffar, she loves Sunil. But it is love and not lust. She does not like her love to be tainted and so she successfull avoids consummation of their love. She says: "I thought unconsummated personal love was the epitome of nobility. I now se there are reaches nobler than unconsummated love." (322)

During the conference of All India 'Khadi Bhandar' worker in Bombay, Rehna suggests that the spinning wheel be put i the Congress flag. All the delegates give their approval to it and shout "onward to freedom through the wheel." Rehna's irrepressible desire is death by water. It is fulfilled when she is killed in the landslide caused by heavy rain at Naini Tal.

Among the British characters, Dyer is cast in the role of a villain and an eternal foe of the Indians. Though born and brought up in India, he is full of hatred for the Indians and says that they deserve to be thrown to the wolves. He did not like the British wasting money on the health facilities in India. He believes that if Indians lived longer, they would not be grateful to the British but they would only use their scheming minds to plot against their rulers.

Dyer hated more the way the Indian towns are built. He says each town is "a web of intricate narrow alleys and alleyways" and full of dung-heaps. He thinks that many times the British suffered defeat because they were ignorant of intricate patterns of these towns. Dyer is seen at his worst on the day of Jallianwala Bagh tragedy. Though Dyer's hatred for the Indians knows no bounds, he has a soft corner for Indian women. As he does not like to hurt his wife, he refrains from fathering a child with an Indian woman himself.

While making a comparison between Kenneth Ashby and Dyer, K. Radha rightly observes: "In contrast to General Dyer, a vampire thirsting for the blood of the Indians, we have the sedate and sensible ICS Officer, Kenneth Ashby who is a creation of Nahal."[13] Kenneth Ashby is aware that though the Indian masses are poor, innocent, trusting and undemanding, they have sense of honour. So he is sympathetic towards them. He says that Indians must get freedom but only through the good will of the British government. But he is one with Dyer in his estimate of Gandhi. He calls Gandhi "a seditious rogue."

Celia Ashby is the American aunt of Kenneth Ashby. With her open mind, she provides an objective estimate of India, non-violent struggle and terrorists. As a result, her character acquires thematic importance. Making a bonfire of foreign goods as part of the national movement surprises her. She has neither seen nor heard of this kind of protest. Seeing the enthusiasm of the people, she senses danger to the existence of British government in

India. Soon, she is infected by the enthusiasm of the participants. She throws off her hat into the fire and encourages the nearby people to keep the bonfire burning.

When the police try to disperse the agitators with water cannons, some of the people standing there only laugh at the drenched women and do not resist. Touched to the quick, she says: "Only why wouldn't you get up and fight back, kick your adversaries? Has a mere two hundred years of British rule made you that docile?" (197) Celia Ashby has an open mind and is not committed to any ideology. She evinces equal interest in learning about the ideology of the revolutionary group, Himmat, from Rakesh. She takes the risk of following Rakesh, a stranger, for the same purpose. She understands that Rakesh and other revolutionaries are no less patriotic than the followers of Gandhi. She has sympathy for them but is sceptical of their success:

> They had mismanaged the 1857 Mutiny, and in all probability would mismanage another one. . . . For the British are so much stronger and well organized. Whereas the average Indian tends to be too humble, too docile. (201)

But she adds that the American war of revolution was an armed rebellion, and like most Americans she wishes Rakesh success. Rakesh is moved by her words. He is aware that there are some "foreign sympathizers of the Indian cause; the Indian National Congress itself was founded by a Britisher. Yet he had seen no foreigner openly act on behalf of the Indians in that fashion—and a woman, at that." (205)

Celia Ashby has a word of praise for the British for having introduced democratic institutions. But at the same time she condemns the callous attitude of the government towards the people when they are suffering under the impact of successive famines and for neglecting irrigation projects. The government's step-motherly treatment of the Eurasians angers her. But it is surprising to see Celia Ashby spending a lot of time in trying to "reform" Spindle, her dog. Her interest in Spindle, in the public burning of foreign clothes and satyagraha appears to be childish to Kenneth Ashby. He asks her to stop jesting. Indeed, she provides variety and comic relief to some extent.

Nahal employs a variety of narrative modes in the novel. To describe Gandhi's retrospective evaluation of his work and life in South Africa, Nahal makes use of the flashback technique. Shakeel Ahmed says: "The use of memory as an artistic implement weds this method to poetry. It enables the writer to place himself at the top of all events, viewing all that leads back to the bottom from a distance, and, thereby, achieve an aesthetic distance."[14]

While describing Gandhi's encounter with the apparitions the two girl inmates of the Tolstoy Farm, his eldest son, Harilal, his elder brother Laxmidas, Hermann Kallenbach, Mir Alam and Valliamma, Nahal makes use of the technique of dramatic narration. He successfully employs the technique of stream of consciousness to recount "the flowing or jagged sequence of thoughts, perceptions, preconscious associations, memories, half-realized impressions"[15] of Sunil who is in a state of semi-consciousness as a result of bullet injury:

> The faces that came to him were the unknown faces he had passed by the roadside, the places too were the unfamiliar places he had gone by. He saw a young mother hugging an infant. . . . He saw an old man with a lump in his throat . . . He saw women weeping and beating their shrunken breasts . . . he was unconscious, his consciousness did not lose the sense of consciousness. A sightless, soundless, action continued in his mind . . . he had sacrificed his life in love only. He couldn't think of the man for whom he had done that. (438-40)

Nahal gives a realistic account of India, both political and social, in the 1920s. He narrates in detail the prevailing Sikh-Hindu-Muslim unity and the impact of the national movement led by Gandhi on family life. When Gandhi asks them to observe hartal in protest against the inhuman and brutal Rowlatt Laws, people from all walks of life respond as one person and display their solidarity. They not only observe hartal but also mass fast for twenty-four hours. In the end, "they broke their bread together, drank water out of the same container and embraced each other in streets. And the police felt powerless." (56) The communal sit-down meal at the time of important ceremonies is another manifestation of their unity. Gandhi succeeds in bringing the whole nation under one umbrella.

Even on ordinary days, Sunil, Muzaffar and others gather at Muzaffar's house and share food, exchange riddles and discuss various things. But towards the end of the novel, the bonhomie that has been prevailing among the different communities is eroded. The result is the formation of the Muslim League and sowing of the seeds of separatism. Some of the Muslims, like Muzaffar, leave the Congress and join the Muslim League.

The realization on the part of many people of the need to eradicate untouchability and put an end to the humiliating treatment being meted out to them presents the seamy side of the impact of the national movement led by Gandhi. But the same movement leads to the disintegration of big families and separation among the members of family:

> The non-cooperation movement and jail-going had completely upset the family clock of many married households. Husbands were in and wives were out or wives were in and husbands were out. Husbands were in one prison and wives in another. . . . Their children were at the mercy of relatives—very often *unwilling* relatives . . . a government servant was immediately dismissed if involved in the movement and others too lost their source of income. The Congress would pay no allowance to the dependents; in a mass movement, the burden must be borne by the masses themselves. . . . Many families totally broke up under the tension. (441)

Chaman Nahal's use of language in the novel is noteworthy. His diction is remarkably simple but it very effectively conveys the thought. Commenting on the British who are under the illusion that they have conquered the Indians, Nahal says:

> Did the English really believe they had *conquered* the Indians? They might have a temporary advantage over them, but had they crushed their convictions? Even the man who pulled the sahib's punkha subscribed to them, howsoever secretively. And how could you hold a nation by the sword? You could destroy by the sword, maim by the sword, keep mouths shut by the sword, but could you change hearts by the sword? (29)

While describing Gandhi's perception, Nahal says: "They did not know Gandhi, though—what a sifter of human beings he was. He had the jeweller's instinct for the precious stone, or the wine-taster's nose for the rich vintage." (143)

One more instance of Nahal's remarkably precise choice of words can be found in his description of spinning as the "new language" every Indian peasant must be taught. Gandhi asks Sunil:

> I'm really asking you to learn a new language. A language that might touch the chord of an Indian peasant everywhere in any corner of India. And once they follow you in spinning, they will follow you in everything, including politics. (143)

While Celia Ashby and Rakesh are talking, Shyama hears the words violence and British. Though her knowledge of English is poor, she guesses the topic they are discussing. She joins them saying: "He [her husband] wrong. Violence wrong. . . . No. Violence evil. . . . My brother, Sunil, his cause better." (206-7) Thus Nahal gives a distinct touch to the character of Shyama.

While describing the dangerous lives the revolutionaries lead, Nahal writes: "Being wiped out was the privilege with which the revolutionaries came into the field. They carried their coffins on their head." (394)

Nahal's choice of epithets to describe the various leaders is indeed marvellous as evidenced in the following lines:

> the mercurial Jawaharlal and the self-possessed Vallabhbhai Patel? . . . the earthy Rajendra Prasad . . . the scholarly Rajagopalachari . . . the fastidious Abul Kalam . . . the humble Kripalani. (143)

Another noteworthy feature of Nahal's language is the description of Punjabi riddles and recitation of couplets. Some of the riddles are:

> Running fast, I fall
> Standing still, I fly in the skies. (174)
>
> The tree is one, but leaves of two types
> Black and white, black and white. (159)

These riddles are known for their romance and repartee.

Nahal, now and then, writes very long sentences. While describing the Rajputs who are moneylenders turned 'zamindars,' he uses a long sentence running into nineteen lines (53-54). Similarly the novelist gives a vivid picture of the picnic lunch Sunil, Muzaffar, Rehna and Kusum had on the snowy mountain at Naini Tal in a very long sentence of twenty-nine lines (312-13)

Nahal's lengthy description of Celia Ashby's attempts to befriend the dog, Spindle, is a satire on the richmen's fad of spending a lot of time and money on pets (184-88). To show that life is full of paradoxes, Nahal makes Rakesh, the revolutionary who is bent upon destroying the system that has been exploiting the poor, fall in love with Shyama, the daughter of Thakur Shanti Nath, "a cog in the system."

Nahal makes an effective use of the form of speech, irony, in the novel. It is ironical to see Dyer calling Gandhi: "The man was crooked, or rather—and Dyer went back to his favourite word—scheming, yes, scheming." (92) The British, after the Jallianwala Bagh massacre, hail Dyer "as a redeemer!" The loyalist, Thakur Shanti Nath believes that the British cannot openly advocate independence for India because "they are too attached to India!" It is ironical to see Kusum joining Gandhi, "the man

. . . who has seized her husband and taken him away from her, who had created a rival for her in her life, who had led her husband to his death." (462)

Yet another instance of irony in the novel is the plantation workers, who are being humiliated as untouchables, themselves practising untouchability: "Here was a man complaining about victimization and was himself hell-bent on victimizing." (235)

Nahal employs a simile to describe Priti, who comes to Sunil, who has been eagerly waiting to meet her: "And she came to him in the night like a mass of burning lava." (245)

Besides the stylistic devices irony and paradox, Nahal successfully employs the technique of contrast in *The Crown and the Loincloth*. While Dyer, who is born in India, calls India, Indians, its landscape, seasons, climate and its cities treacherous, Kenneth Ashby, a British ICS officer "had fallen somewhat in love with the people of the land. They were so trusting, so undemanding. What a sense of humour they had—in spite of the poverty." (98) Nahal also contrasts the organized violence of the revolutionaries with the organized non-violence advocated by Gandhi and his followers.

In spite of his ability to use language very effectively, Nahal admits its inadequacies: "From magic to wonder to pity. How inadequate was language to convey shades of human experience! You never conveyed exactly what you wanted." (337)

It is interesting to note that Nahal refers to Gandhi as Mohandas in the first chapter of the first part of the novel. But in the following pages, Nahal refers to him as Gandhi.

The title of the novel suggests that the dominating symbols of the novel are the crown and the loincloth. The crown represents the British government and loincloth Gandhi. They denote the conflict between the alien, repressive and unwanted government and the national movement for freedom led by Gandhi. After protracted self-examination, Gandhi decides to purify himself further and lead the nation against the government. Then, Nahal symbolically suggests the impending victory of Gandhi by describing "a curious phenomenon":

When the rays of the morning sun struck the deck, the

> portrait [of King George V], which was previously quite clearly visible, went into darkness; it looked as though the frame held only a sheet of glass and a blankness behind it. And the same rays conspicuously lit up the man in the loincloth, casting a beam on him. (42-43)

When Gandhi is sentenced to six years's imprisonment on charges of sedition, Nahal writes: "For the time being, the lion in loincloth was caged." (466)

Thus, in *The Crown and the Loincloth*, Nahal concentrates on the period—1915-1922—during which the people greatly influenced by Gandhi's idealism, unitedly oppose the alien government by offering satyagraha, by observing hartals and by boycotting foreign goods and the visit of the Prince of Wales. Nahal also shows how under the tremendous influence of Gandhi, Sunil believes in the policy of non-violent resistance and begins to work for the eradication of untouchability. While describing how the independence movement progressed under the leadership of Gandhi, Nahal displays his skill in creating living characters and in making good use of various literary devices like irony, satire and contrast. Nahal's diction and fascination for writing long sentences compel our attention. The novel reveals not only Nahal's exquisite narrative technique but also his skill in blending fact and fiction.

NOTES

1. Chaman Nahal, *The Crown and the Loincloth* (New Delhi: Vikas, 1981), vol. 1 of *The Gandhi Quartet* (New Delhi: Allied, 1993), p. 38.
2. Ian Milligan, *The Novel in English: An Introduction* (Hampshire: Macmillan, 1987), p. 115.
3. M.K. Naik, "Gandhiji and Indian Writing in English," *Critical Essays on Indian Writing in English*. ed. M.K. Naik et al (1968; Madras: Macmillan, 1977), p. 370.
4. H.M. Nayak, *Gandhiji in Indian Literature* (Mysore: University of

Mysore, 1971), p. 7.

5. Bhabani Bhattacharya, *Mahatma Gandhi* (1977; New Delhi: Arnold Heinemann, 1982), p. 10.
6. Chandra Shanker Shukla, *Gandhi's View of Life* (Bombay: Bharatiya Vidya Bhavan, 1956), p. 79.
7. J.B. Kripalani, *The Gandhian Way* (Bombay: Vora, 1938), p. 171.
8. Aldous Huxley, "Non-Violence," *Choice and Master Spirits*, ed. C.A. Sheppard (New Delhi: Orient Longman, 1976), p. 56.
9. C.E.M. Joad, "The Gandhian Way," *Contemporary English Prose*, ed. Hari Singh and T.C. Balakrishna Menon (Bombay: Blackie, 1976), p. 2.
10. Daisaku Ikeda, *Toward a World without War: Gandhism and the Modern World* (New Delhi: Gandhi Smriti and Darshan Samiti, 1992), p. 17.
11. K.R. Srinivasa Iyengar, rev. of *The Crown and the Loincloth*, *The Literary Criterion*, 16.3 (1981), p. 77.
12. *Ibid.*, p. 78.
13. K. Radha, "The English in *Azadi* and *The Crown and the Loincloth*," *Three Contemporary Novelists*, ed. R.K. Dhawan (New Delhi: Classical, 1985), p. 158.
14. Shakeel Ahmad, *The Theoretical Viability of the Flashback Method as Technique of Fiction* (Gaya: New Concept Publications, 1991), pp. 31-34.
15. Bruce F. Kawin, "The Mind of the Text," *The Mind of the Novel* (New Jersey: Princeton University Press, 1982), p. 233.

Enduring Ceaseless Suffering: *The Salt of Life*

After describing the first mass movement led by Gandhi and his awareness of the necessity to make the people fearless so that another Chauri Chaura may be averted, Chaman Nahal continues the Gandhi Saga in *The Salt of Life* (1993) which forms the second volume of *The Gandhi Quartet*. The novel, in the main, deals with the epoch-making Dandi March of Gandhi, his faith in his followers to show the way out when in a crunch and his successful attempts in making women realize their true potential and play a more effective role in the freedom struggle. Nahal also describes the parallel movements in India's struggle for freedom led by Subhas Chandra Bose and Bhagat Singh. Finally, Nahal throws light on the impact of Gandhi and the second mass movement on the social fabric as well as on certain foreign nationals who have been observing Gandhi from close quarters.

Chaman Nahal begins the novel on a negative note. Gandhi in 1929 is overcome by a sense of defeat because people are still going in for foreign goods. Many Hindus and Muslims are still considering each other bitter enemies and untouchability is still being practised. Much to the chagrin of the people, the British are still the rulers of India. So Gandhi wants to find a new vocabulary to "channelize the angry roar of the people properly." He concludes that Salt Satyagraha will be the new vocabulary. And as Tara Chand rightly observes: "The solution of Gandhiji was a stroke of genius. No commander of a military plan of operations could have done better. The Salt Satyagraha had all the elements of high class strategy—surprise, universal mobilization of forces, discipline, organization, simplicity of tactics, universal availability of means and instruments of war, challenging and surrounding the forces of the enemy from all sides, drama."[1]

The success of the civil disobedience movement forces the imperialist government to withdraw the Salt Act. But soon the alien government resorts to the old ways of repressing the people. As a result, gloom spreads everywhere and Gandhi feels that the nationalists have reached the end of the road. At this stage he watches the play, "God or Gandhi." It makes him realize that the only remedy for their suffering is salt, in working hard and enduring suffering till India becomes a free nation.

Parallel to Gandhi's non-violent struggle for freedom, Nahal presents the attempts of Subhas Chandra Bose to secure the help of Japan in freeing India from colonial rule. Bose becomes the choice of the people who are clamouring for an aggressive strike against the government of India. Nahal also presents the attempts of Bhagat Singh and other revolutionaries to teach the unwanted government a lesson or two through violent methods.

While the historical events move round Gandhi, the fictional narrative is centred round Kusum. After marrying Raja Vishal Chand, Kusum leaves her son, Vikram, with Gandhi and accompanies the Raja to Lambini. Later, the Raja abdicates the throne in favour of Amit, his son by Kusum, and goes to Gompha, on a journey of purification of body and mind. There he dies in a mountain accident. Then, Kusum goes to Sevagram seeking solace in the presence of Gandhi. Soon, she learns from Bapu that the need of the hour is not to complain about her suffering but assimilate it by working more as Gandhi has been doing, till the nation gets self-rule.

The novel is neatly structured and its components, plot, theme and form fit together to produce a totality, a satisfying whole.

Chaman Nahal divides the novel into three parts—"Whispers," "Temper" and "Choices." After the first successful mass movement, there is lull on the Indian political scene. Gandhi has no new plan of action to offer to the nation that is groaning under the imperialistic misrule. Still, one can hear whispers of protest against the British government. In the princely state of

Travancore, where direct political activity is prohibited, people invent games symbolizing such activity. After taking a meal, everyone makes a heap of the large plantain leaves on which food is served and set it on fire. Thus, they are making a bonfire of foreign clothes. While stealing a nap at noon, a few rickshaw pullers would keep their rickshaws in a side lane and refuse to take any passengers. They tell the passengers that they are on hartal, on strike:

> Then there was the Kathakali mime in which the dancers wore huge masks and acted out mythological stories in the streets, each such story projecting the downfall of the bad and the evil. The demon was now painted white, wearing blue trousers, and became the tale of a bad white man being hounded out by the good natives.[2]

The government asks Kusum and Raja Vishal Chand to arrest Gandhi, when he reaches Lambini while he is on his way to Lahore. But they outwit the government by advising Gandhi to go to Lahore without touching Lambini. Since then, Kusum goes on hearing "an enormous whisper—more disturbing more imminent than the spoken word." One day, Vishal Chand reads out "the news of the day" aloud to Kusum:

> Gandhiji's resolution on complete independence is adopted by the open session of the Lahore Congress on thirtieth December. Gandhiji leads the midnight pledge for independence taken at Lahore on thirty-first December. (172)

Kusum is alerted and sits up in surprise. Then, once again, she hears the whisper telling her: "This is what I have been trying to tell you, of a new wind of change, of a new storm that is gathering at the horizon." (172) It is evident that it is only a question of time when everyone under the leadership of Gandhi would take the country by storm.

In the second part of the novel, "Tempers," Nahal gives a vivid description of the tempers of the British and their adversaries, Gandhi and his followers during and after the historic

Dandi March. Gandhi is aware that he is marching against the formidable enemy who has no compunction in using force against his non-violent army. Still, he does not feel perturbed. He says, "he would laugh and dance his way to Dandi . . . the goal would be his." The Salt Satyagraha sets the whole country aflame. At several places the Indian police and the army disobey orders and refuse to shoot their fellow Indians. People act as Indians and not as Muslims or Hindus or Sikhs, much to the mortification of the British: "The temper of the present moment, its pace, its rhythm, its momentum was different. It was a faster temper. It was a bolder temper. It was a threatening temper." (263)

Compared with the tempers of Gandhi, Vikram and the satyagrahis, the tempers of Joseph Daniel, a revolutionary, and of the British are violent. Joseph Daniel and his friend blow up the Ugoki Church, where some of the Europeans assemble. The unprecedented success of the second mass movement unnerves the government. It does not honour the Gandhi-Irwin Pact and begins to persecute the peasants and refuses to return the confiscated property. It says even whistling of Vande Mataram is punishable.

In the third part of the novel, "Choices" Nahal says: "The study of history is a study of the alternative choices open to a people at a particular time." (375) During 1930 and 1940, Gandhi, Pakistan, Subhas Bose, and Bhagat Singh are the choices for the people of India. Many choose Gandhi as their leader, take part in the non-violent non-cooperation movement and civil disobedience movement. They suffer a lot for the sake of liberating their country. The Muslim Conference in 1940 declares that it will also fight for a free India but "a free Hindu India as one unit," and "a free Muslim India as the other unit." The third choice open to the people is Subhas Bose, who believes that use of force is inevitable to drive the British out of India. But for the majority of the Indians, Gandhi remains the only choice.

The incidents in *The Salt of Life* are arranged in a logically ordered sequence and they arouse interest and suspense. There is continual interaction between the characters and the incidents portrayed. There are no loose threads. The plot is concerned with the Salt Satyagraha led by Gandhi, its unqualified success, the repression unleashed by the government on the satyagrahis, the miraculous escape of Subhas Bose to Russia, signing of Gandhi-Irwin Pact, Gandhi's participation in the Second Round Table Conference in London, the renewed repression on the freedom fighters, the hanging of Rakesh for his revolutionary activities and Kusum's successful satyagraha against racial prejudice symbolizing a new political awakening among the women of India.

Nahal takes care to see that no character including Gandhi is idealized. He begins the portrayal of Gandhi on a negative note, thereby making it clear that he has no intention of idealizing Gandhi. Gandhi is seized with a sense of defeat and disappointment because India is still reeling under the repressive regime. His efforts to eradicate untouchability and make the Hindus and Muslims live in amity have not borne fruit. The spinning wheel over the years has become a mere status symbol. Many, including Jawaharlal Nehru, are going in for the finer variety of khadi. The distinction made between finer and coarser varieties of khadi pains Gandhi. In the words of Bhabani Bhattacharya: "he was far in advance of his impulse-ridden times. Or, perhaps, he was too far behind them, a relic from bygone centuries when high ideals prevailed."[3] Consequently, many, including Jawaharlal Nehru and Kasturbai consider him enigmatic. As the monkey menace is on the increase, he decides to kill them with poison. Many 'ashramites' and people living in the nearby villages protest saying that one should not kill the avatar of Hanuman. His disapproval of the violent methods adopted by Bhagat Singh and his comrades draws flak from many including some of his associates.

Nahal hastens to add that though many people have failed to comprehend Gandhi's ideology, they have unflinching faith in him as their leader by pointing out their readiness "to do his bidding." Gandhi is moved by their faith in him and reciprocates their faith by having affection and regard for everyone of them. He listens to Kusum telling her students how to make salt. It reminds him of the British monopoly on the manufacture of salt in India. It is unjust on the part of the British to impose tax on salt that savours millions of poor people's half a meal a day:

> Salt is another name for honour, for dignity, for patriotism, for valour. The British have eaten the food that is grown here. Yet they have not quite eaten the salt of India, as they are scared of it. . . . The British have made it difficult for the average Indian to eat the salt of his own land unless he first pays a cut or tax to these invaders. (46)

He decides to oppose it by launching an agitation and it will be his "new vocabulary." It will articulate the resentment against the colonial rule.

Gandhi's Salt Satyagraha is startling in its concept. It is as simple as it is unusual, but unmistakably logical and unprecedented: "Oftentimes did he say that he saw no light and was praying for it. And when he sees the light it appears strange to his people, for his remedies are unprecedented and awe-inspiring."[4]

As he begins his historic march to Dandi on 12 March 1930, his inner voice tells him that he has taken the right decision. So a thin smile of impending triumph spreads on his face. And this makes Nahal present yet another facet of Gandhi's personality, his concern for the downtrodden. Even in such a happy state of mind, Gandhi does not forget his duty to the neglected sections of society. He declares that he will go on a pilgrimage not to the Himalayas but to the places where people are being segregated and humiliated. Further, he wants to find God not by meditating in a remote ashram in the Himalayas but in action. He reaches Dandi on 5 April after a 240 mile march. He is greeted by 75,000 people on the sands of Sabarmati who pledge allegiance to him. He picks a lump of salt and violates the law. Ingenious as he always is, he asks the people in other parts of the country to go to the sea-shore nearest to them, pick up some grains of salt and thus defy the government. People everywhere obey Gandhi like disciplined soldiers. Though the policemen rain blows on their heads, they do not even raise an arm to fend off the blows. As Louis Fisher puts it: "The British beat the Indians with batons and rifle butts. The Indians neither cringed nor complained or retreated. That made England powerless and India invincible."[5]

The resounding success of the Salt Satyagraha reveals the impact of Gandhi on his countrymen. Equally significant is his influence on certain foreign nationals and even on political adversaries. Carol Schnicke of Australia realizes that the only way to get peace in life is to help the needy. So she starts an ashram on the lines of Gandhi's Sabarmati Ashram and provides shelter to the physical and mental wrecks. When some Hindu fundamentalists deny Matthew Craig, an American, entry into a temple, he offers satyagraha and succeeds in securing entry into the temple. Though Bhagat Singh opposes Gandhi over the methods to be adopted in liberating the country, he holds Bapu in utmost regard.

Nahal reveals Gandhi's ability to foresee the mischief the British are playing, their attempts to institutionalize religion and divide India. As he visualizes, Jinnah throws a spanner into Gandhi's efforts to keep the Hindus and Muslims united by demanding a separate state for Muslims. His failure to wean Jinnah away from the two nation theory, makes Gandhi disappointed.

This leads the novelist to present yet another facet of Gandhi's personality. He has the capacity to remain unruffled, genial and calm even in the midst of a stormy situation. He takes pleasure in seeing the play "God or Gandhi." While others think that he has been wasting time over such trifles, Gandhi learns valuable things from it. After seeing the show, he understands what he should do in the none-too-happy situation. Ten years ago he marched to Dandi thinking that it was the panacea for the ills of India. But it only resulted in more repression. Till date he has not come out with a new course of action. After seeing the show "God or Gandhi" he realizes that the ultimate remedy lies in salt only in that they must endure "ceaseless suffering" till India gains independence.

Nahal's admirable portrayal of Jawaharlal Nehru clearly brings out the latter's idealism, concern for the welfare of his countrymen, frankness and love of discipline. Nehru joins the Indian freedom struggle on the suggestion of Gandhi. Soon, he becomes a popular leader and draws huge crowds wherever he goes. He has high regard for Gandhi.

Impressed by the tremendous progress made by the Soviet Union within a short span of a decade, Nehru begins to dream of converting India, a poor agrarian country, into a power to be reckoned with. He comes out with long term plans to realize his dreams even before India becomes a free nation. He tells Gandhi that his India of the future is an industrial, scientific, socialist India "free of cant and superstition." Between Nehru and Gandhi there is "not unoften, serious disputation on fundamental matters."[6] Nehru wants to reform the Mahatma so that the latter becomes more rational and scientific. However, "over issues of great moment, he would yield to his master, rejoicing, as it were, in a spiritual thraldom that he could not always entirely justify to himself."[7] As a result, the revolutionaries hold him in contempt. They consider him the "willing man of Gandhi."

Though a liberal, Jawaharlal Nehru is a man of principles. Nahal illustrates this by narrating the incident in the Lahore Central Jail. When Nehru goes to meet Bhagat Singh, the latter and his followers raise slogans: "Inqilab, Zindabad!" "Long live revolution!" "Bharat Mata ki Jai!" (81) Nehru takes them to task and admonishes them not to resort to slogan mongering, which breaks their promise made to jail authorities not to indulge in such things. He admires Bhagat Singh's honesty and sincerity. However, he firmly tells them that if Bhagat Singh is guilty of cognizable offences, he must suffer punishment for them.

The call of Mother India to free her from the fetters of the alien government makes many people give up their lucrative jobs and join the freedom movement. Subhas Bose is one among them. He resigns from ICS and plunges headlong into the struggle for freedom. He becomes the President of the Congress in 1938. This born rebel firmly believes that it will take very long time to win freedom through Gandhian methods. So he tells Gandhi and Jawaharlal Nehru that "the struggle for freedom might have to take on a global thrust." But as Gandhi and Nehru "balk at Bose's phraseology," he parts company with the Congress in 1939 and forms Forward Block with the goal of achieving socialism and freedom without delay. Hiren Mukherjee rightly observes: "Subhas had an excess of natural ardour, was uniquely capable of courage and sacrifice, drawn towards ideology, but with the practical man's impatience of it, zealous of what may be called the military virtues which he thought would hasten achievement of his over-mastering and excessive desire, the freedom of India." (82-83)

Subhas Bose's belief that a third country like Germany or Japan will help India win freedom without any ulterior motive shows that his bubbling enthusiasm and patriotism are not matched by pragmatism. However, during the freedom struggle, Subhas Bose produced another choice apart from Gandhi's non-violent struggle to the freedom fighters.

While Gandhi and Nehru opt for peaceful means, Subhas Bose and Bhagat Singh adopt violent methods to break the fetters of alien rule and liberate India. The revolutionaries, in their turn, follow different methods in their efforts to realize their dream of driving the British imperialists out of India. Subhas Bose decides to take the help of either Germany or Japan and strike at the government in India from outside the country. But Bhagat Singh becomes a terrorist.

Bhagat Singh is young, energetic, "absolutely seething and burning." Like Subhas Chandra Bose, he believes in physically forcing the British to leave India. He is after Scott, whose lathi blows caused the death of Lala Lajpat Rai. But he only succeeds in killing Saunders, another Englishman instead of Scott. Bhagat Singh enriches the vocabulary of the revolutionaries by adding the word "speed" to "revenge." He believes that they must act quickly. He suspects that "Gandhi is essentially a bourgeois renegade and thereby an ally of the British against the poor. All his talk of sympathy for teeming millions of India was bullshit, nothing but *talk*." (57) So he believes that "the poor had to stick together and come out with their own platform of protest, their own symbolic gestures." (57)

Disenchanted with Gandhi, Bhagat Singh starts a new political party, Hindustan Socialist Republican Party, and becomes its General Secretary. Accompanied by his follower, Charulata, he throws a bomb in the Legislative Assembly in New Delhi on 8 April 1929. As it is done only as a "protest of the poor," no one is killed or hurt in the incident. Still, he is sentenced to death along with Charulata. But he is happy because the bomb throwing incident "accomplished its task: It made even Gandhi sit back and search his conscience." (58) So he declares that he and his followers will not escape from the prison. In spite of his disapproval of the violent methods adopted by Bhagat Singh, Gandhi admires the former's commitment to the cause of freedom. He calls Bhagat Singh "a great son of India."

Nahal takes care to present even minor characters like Sheik Abdullah in their true colours. A leader of the Muslim Conference, Sheik Abdullah is thin, handsome and forbidding. He does in Kashmir what Gandhi and the Congress have been doing in other parts of India, "to take them [the Kashmiris] towards the same freedom and egalitarianism which the rest of India was demanding." (402)

As soon as he comes to know of the selling of the Muslim girls, he launches a movement against the slave market. All the native Muslims join him. They squat on the roads, "cut off communications and mobility." Like a seasoned sleuth, he gathers all the details about the involvement of Percy Wand and Jennifer Wand in the nefarious activity. He pricks the bubble of the infalliability of the British by proving that Percy Wand is insane and a sexual pervert. He succeeds in making the Maharaja of Kashmir punish the guilty Indians involved in the slave market.

Nahal's portrayal of Kasturbai shows that Gandhi remains an enigmatic person even to his wife. Her failure to understand Gandhi's personality and motives behind his actions, makes her his severest critic. When Gandhi declares that he is a true democrat, Ba says: "It meant the acceptance of *his* word, *his* law, *his* rule. He kept the discussion going until his audience was worn out to the point of exhaustion and then submitted to whatever he wanted." (15) But she does not seem to know the truth that Gandhi is only trying to visualize his thoughts for his benefit.

Similarly, she fails to understand Gandhi when he rebukes her for not having deposited a "small gift of four rupees" with the cashier and writes a "two-page harangue" against her in *Young India.* Instead of repenting for what she has done, she questions Gandhi whether he is justified in killing of a maimed calf in the ashram. Evidently, she fails to understand that Gandhi agreed to the mercy killing of calf because it had no chance of survival. He actually put an end to its pain.

Ba betrays her ignorance on yet another occasion when Gandhi faints in a prayer meeting. When Kusum thinks that he has gone into 'samadhi' and is in communion with God, Ba says that it is only the deed of "a clever merchant." At times, she thinks that he is no better than "a grown up baby in a pram." Despite her failure to understand Gandhi's enigmatic personality, she always serves him with love, affection and regard. Gandhi himself admits it.

Nahal presents even British characters like Churchill convincingly. He effectively brings out the dichotomy between the words and deeds of the British rulers and their chauvinism in his portrayal of Winston Churchill. Churchill declares: "We are for the freedom of every nation." But he immediately adds that freedom will be granted to India only when "the patchwork of communities" that are in India rise to the level of a nation. He adds that he has not become the Prime Minister of England to liquidate the British empire. When he sees the photograph showing Jennifer Wand trying to stab Cutlass, he comments: "Ah, where indeed is the good old British character today! It's a sad day indeed when the only valour a Britisher can show is in attacking a fellow Britisher." (500) He feels that the need of the hour is to resurrect the British character so that it will revive their image and help Britain come out victorious in the war. As part of the image-building exercise, he dismisses Percy Wand, Jennifer's brother, from service, decides to reward the Indian loyalists, and severely punish the freedom fighters.

Raja Vishal Chand is presented as one who stands out among the heads of princely states with his individuality, regard for Gandhi and his precepts. As the ruler of Lambini, he frees his tenants, distributes their holdings to them and makes them owners of the land they till. He fixes a salary for himself and becomes the only salaried 'raja' in the whole of India. On Gandhi's advice, he starts co-educational schools. All this endears him to the people of Lambini. He is so religious that he neither allows his people to kneel before him nor is he willing to kneel before others: "The religious man in him believed only in one durbar—of God. He had long since abolished durbars in his state. . . . No, the religious man in him couldn't possibly kneel before anyone except the Almighty." (142) So he is not willing to build a palace representing Lambini near the feet of the Viceroy's Palace in Delhi. Instead, he allows the Congress to hold an exhibition in that land. He insists on everyone addressing him as "Raja Saheb" and not as "Your Highness" or "Exalted Highness."

Though he has a loving wife, a dutiful son and a large number of admirers, Raja Vishal Chand begins to feel discontented. He realizes that the time has come for him to cleanse his mind and spirit. So he abdicates his throne to his son, Amit, and goes to Gompah, the Buddhist monastery, to attend the annual initiation ceremony. From there, he goes alone to have a look at the Mount Kailash. But there, he dies in mysterious circumstances. However, he looks dignified even in death, never giving "the impression of a corpse." All the same, Nahal is not blind to the darker side of Raja Vishal Chand's character. With all his nobility, he lacks self-control. When he meets Kusum in Sabarmati, he falls in love with her. He loves her so passionately, that he makes love to her before marriage, violating ashram vows.

Another interesting minor character in the novel is Hemant Kumar, an eminent criminal lawyer who seems to have been modelled on Motilal Nehru. He is respected not only by other lawyers but also by the judges: "The judges were most deferential to him and it was seldom that an 'objection, Your Honour,' raised by him was not sustained by them." (442) In recognition of his eminence as a lawyer the government appoints him as a judge and confers the title, Rai Bahadur on him. Though he refuses to become a judge, he accepts the title, Rai Bahadur. His loyalty to the legal system evolved by the British makes him accept without protest the death sentence passed on his son,

Rakesh, for his revolutionary activities. However, he comes to realize the hypocrisy of the British only during the Second World War. He agrees that Gandhi is right in his assertion that British have two sets of laws, one for their own consumption and the other for the people they governed. He asks: "If the British today were fighting the Germans for their right to exist, how could they deny the same right to the Indians?" (443) So he changes his mind and concludes that Rakesh was justified in becoming a revolutionary and in trying to assassinate the Prince of Wales who represented the oppressive regime. He makes a valiant but vain attempt to save his son from the gallows.

Equally fascinating is the character of Vikram, who is greatly influenced by Gandhi. Vikram's seven-year-stay in Sabarmati makes him "a little saint." He proudly says, "It's not my mother who has brought me up. It's Bapu." (126) Consoling Abha after she was lost and found at the fair at Trivandrum, he tells her, "you have to meet Bapu to come out of your shell." (128) Vikram refuses the luxurious life offered by his new father Raja Vishal Chand and takes part in Salt Satyagraha. In fact, he leads Gandhi by holding his staff all the way to Dandi. The newspapers carry his photograph and soon he becomes a legend. In spite of an injury on his head, he boldly resists the police who come to arrest Gandhi. His bandaged head becomes a symbol of India's tenacity. Even though he is young, he realizes the importance of the virtue of non-possession. When Raja Vishal Chand decides to abdicate his throne, he observes that the Raja is only getting rid of his burden. The impact of Gandhi on Vikram is such that Vikram's mind, soul and even his dreams hover round Gandhi. So he goes away to Nagpur to conduct a Youth Camp without waiting to console his mother who is widowed for the second time.

In India's struggle for freedom, the revolutionaries who have made significant contributions were in thousands. Some of them are Veer Savarkar, Chandra Shekhar Azad and Ras Behari Bose. But as Satyavrata Ghosh rightly observes: "Those who worked in the Open Wing of our Freedom Movement had the emotional compensation of fame and fanfare, while the revolutionaries were completely denied of them. If, following Milton, we accept that, 'fame is the last infirmity of noble mind,' they had hardly any."[8] Evidently, Nahal modelled the fictional characters Rakesh Kumar and Joseph Daniel on such revolutionaries.

The revolutionaries are no less patriotic than Gandhi and his followers. But while Gandhi tries to persuade the British to quit India, the revolutionaries want to take revenge on the alien rulers. For the revolutionaries it is the end and not the means that matters. Rakesh Kumar is one of the members of the revolutionary outfit, Himmat. After his abortive attempt to kill the Prince of Wales, he has to abandon his loving wife and only child and seek shelter in far away places. It makes him sad. Still, he accepts the difficult task of entering the impregnable Lahore Central Jail and help Bhagat Singh and Charulata escape. He befriends some disgruntled Eurasian jail officials and enters the jail. But as Bhagat Singh and his comrades refuse to escape, Rakesh leaves the jail alone. Later, he disguises himself as Subhas Bose, diverts the attention of the authorities and thereby helps Subhas Bose flee India.

But his dangerous living and loneliness force Rakesh to seek comfort from the Goan mistresses and liquor. It makes his life slovenly and commonplace. When he wants to meet his daughter, Abha, whom he sees after a very long time, Kusum prevents him from meeting her. Kusum tells him that it would rock the boat of his wife Shyama's life, who is now married to Zahir. As there is nothing to live for, Rakesh immediately surrenders to the police.

Nahal, thus, vividly describes the touching lives of the revolutionaries. As the government wants to punish them for their violent deeds, they flee their homes to escape punishment. While the non-violent method of protest of Gandhi and his followers enables them to openly oppose the government, the revolutionaries have to abandon their families and live a hazardous life.

Joseph Daniel, one of the founder members of the Himmat, is ingenious. He is the brain behind every move the revolutionaries make. He suggests to Rakesh to disguise himself as Subhas Bose, mislead the government and help Subhas Bose reach Kabul. Joseph Daniel's strong desire is to keep the Himmat strong by recruiting youngsters. He does not hesitate to adopt even devious methods to succeed in this. He notices that Naval is interested in the writings of Prem Chand. Saying that he will introduce him to that eminent writer, Joseph Daniel inveigles him into the organisation.

Like other revolutionaries, he resolves to take revenge on the government that does not have the approval of the natives. When he learns that many British officers have gathered at the Ugoki Church, he succeeds in putting it on fire. However, he is disappointed to find that none of the agents of British imperialism have perished in the fire. But he consoles himself saying that he has caused discomfiture to the alien government.

As Srinivasa Iyengar rightly observes: "The *Quartet* is Gandhi's story, India's story; It is also Kusum's story."[9] If the historical narrative centres around Gandhi, the fictional narrative is dominated by Kusum. Nahal shows her repudiating the centuries-old ugly Indian tradition of confining a widow to the kitchen. After the death of her husband, Sunil, she retires with her son, Vikram, to Sabarmati and thus makes her own affirmation. She begins to work as a teacher in the ashram school. She introduces Basic Education, which Gandhi admits, he had never thought of. When Raja Vishal Chand with his passionate love for her, gives her relief and restores feminity and dignity, she yields to him. She violates the ashram vows and becomes pregnant. She does not repent her action because "she yielded, submitted herself so totally, to a man, to a cause, to an idea." (103) However, she does not like to lose her identity. When Raja Vishal Chand says that he has met his mother in Kusum, she protests saying, "I am not her, though, I am myself." (91)

Though a follower of Gandhi, Kusum does not consider happiness a morally suspect word. When she learns that Shyama has married a wine merchant, Zahir, Kusum is not shocked. On the other hand, she is happy because Zahir has brought Shyama protection and happiness. Kusum is aware that nobility bestows glory upon one: "It was in search of that fragile solace that the Hindu women observed their fasts, went on pilgrimages, or burned themselves at pyres of their dead husbands." (102) But she has "altogether broken with that web of delusions."

Later, the "inanities," "insults" and "lies" mouthed by Percy Wand bring out the rebel in her. Nahal uses the archetypal image of 'Shakti' (the goddess of Strength) to bring out the rebellious spirit in her. She squats on the track and does not allow the prestigious Frontier Mail to leave Wazirabad railway station. Soon, she is joined by many people living in the vicinity of the station and they offer satyagraha. She allows the train to move only when the Commissioner of Lahore Division, Sir Kenneth Ashby, apologizes to her. Even when tragedy strikes her in the form of the death of Raja Vishal Chand, she obeys Bapu by offering a novel mode of individual satyagraha, a sit-in, protesting against the misrule of the government. Thus, she proves herself to be "a woman who had continually elevated herself; her life had been an upward progression of the spirit—all the way." (495)

Though endowed with feminist traits, Kusum, at times, behaves like an ordinary woman. The reason seems to be Nahal's intention not to deify her. She is not able to forget that she has been neglected by her first husband, Sunil, and son, Vikram. She accuses Gandhi of not being compassionate to her, who is widowed for the second time and says:

> No, we are just as many hands for your movement, as many witless workers. We may be witless, but we have a private self too—all of us. You conveniently forget that. (527)

But Gandhi tells her, with tears rolling down his cheeks, that he suffers with and for his followers. The need of the hour is to assimilate suffering and continue the national struggle for freedom from the oppressive regime. These words of Gandhi give her a true perspective of the situation. Then, she declares that she will not lament "what's come to pass." Thus, she makes an "affirmation in acceptance."

The young Shyama is presented as a hot-blooded and selfish woman. Though she and Rakesh are ideologically poles apart, she elopes with him. After his unsuccessful attempt to kill the Prince of Wales, Rakesh goes into hiding for seven long years.

At this stage, she meets Zahir, who promises to save her "from gloom." So she embraces Islam and marries him. But she does not tell Abha, her daughter by Rakesh, about him for fear that it would disturb her happy and quiet life. But her selfishness gives place to compassion when she learns that Rakesh is going to be hanged.

Abha's life shows how the struggle for self-rule results in the displacement of people and forces them seek a new identity. When her mother marries Zahir, embraces Islam and starts living in Trivandrum, Abha feels like a fish out of water. Abha, who is very young, finds it very difficult to forget her native place and kith and kin. She asks herself: "Yes, what had happened to her world? Where had it gone? Where was Nana? Where was the haveli?" (96) Their language and mode of dressing looks funny to her. She is surprised to see a stranger moving closely with her mother. She wonders: "Had they kidnapped her and her mother and brought them here? Was she a captive?" (96)

As a result of the clash between the fond memories of her earlier life and the new and strange surroundings, she is estranged from her mother. She always remains aloof from her. She hates her new father. She is sad that she does not remember her father.

Later, when Percy Wand tells her of his father and his revolutionary activities, she is happy that he has to abandon family for a cause and she is proud that he is going to die for the same cause. When she learns of the sale of girls, she boldly offers satyagraha defying the authorities. Though young and lonely, Abha, unlike her mother, learns to live for a cause.

Nahal gives a magnificent insight into British character and stresses the Britishers's inability to communicate with the Indians, which leads to their ultimate drifting away from India. Still, they are not prepared to go back to England. They continue to stay in India because India gave them a chance to live like a ruling class to which very few of them really belonged. For their existence in India, they convert the tradition, which upheld their rule earlier, into a weapon to destroy all established values. Nahal illustrates this through the portrayal of Percy Wand.

Percy Wand is a British political service officer. His forefathers came to India "in the hope of quick gains." But they failed to realize their dream of becoming rich. Still, as they have nothing but "neglect and poverty" back in England, they stayed on in India. However, their prolonged stay in India fails to appease Percy Wand and his half-sister, Jennifer Wand.

Percy Wand realizes that soon the British Raj in India will come to an end. So he tells his sister that

> the only way to dodge a hostile fate is to be hostile yourself. Be hostile, be aggressive, be outrageous, be on the offensive. If only I—if only we—could do something really preposterous, really outlandish. Then we will be one up on this barbarous fate. (152)

His behaviour becomes really outrageous. He becomes a sexual pervert and begins to abuse young boys. He moves so closely with his sister that people wonder whether they are lovers. But he does nothing to curb the gossip. He shocks everyone by declaring that selling of Kashmiri girls to work as concubines, wives and slaves is neither unethical nor illegal. While working in Kashmir, he accumulates a bank balance disproportionate to his known earnings.

Percy Wand is not only corrupt, perverse but also arrogant. He tries to browbeat Raja Vishal Chand into constructing a palace representing Lambini in Delhi. Percy Wand is incompetent too. He mistakes Rakesh, the surrogate Subhas Bose for the real Subhas Bose and follows him. As a result, Subhas Bose succeeds in fleeing India. But the British authorities only ask Percy Wand to resign because "an enquiry would be damaging to the image of all Englishmen." Percy Wand represents the British Raj in its decadent stage in India.

Nahal presents Kenneth Ashby, a British ICS officer, as a foil to Percy Wand. As a result of his long stay in India, Kenneth Ashby comes to love India and Indians. So he allows Angela, his beloved, to work as a teacher at Lambini Public School. Later, he joins Raja Vishal Chand's expedition to the Buddhist monastery at Gompah.

Though Kenneth Ashby is firm in discharging his duties, he is pragmatic. He is aware of the growing opposition to the British rule in India:

> Already the prisons were packed to the full with the political prisoners. . . . How many more prisoners could the jails take without becoming meaningless as institutions of penal servitude? If they were filled with political prisoners alone—as many were—they would become—as many had—a nesting ground for further political activity. (293)

So he defuses the explosive situation created by Percy Wand at Wazirabad railway station by acting firmly. He gives a stern warning to Percy Wand that he will have him arrested for breach of peace. But at the same time, he is polite to Kusum. He apologizes to her for the inconvenience caused to her by Percy Wand and succeeds in dispersing the satyagrahis.

Kenneth Ashby's love for Angela brings to mind Shakespeare's description of true love. The poet-dramatist writes:

> Love alters not with his brief hours and weeks,
> But bears it out even to the edge of doom.[10]

Though they meet after twenty long years, their love remains undiminished:

> He [Kenneth Ashby] made a concerted bid to smile but it didn't come on. Angela too made a concerted bid but failed. Yet she nodded her head, closing her lips, her cheeks expanding and puffing under her own stress. She withdrew her hands, put her arms around Ken's neck, and hugged him. The twenty years of wait were encapsulated into those twenty seconds. Angela sobbed and placed her head on Ken's shoulder. (296)

As regards the narrative technique, though Chaman Nahal employs a variety of narrative modes, he depends mostly on the omniscient point of view, in tune with the nature of the subject matter he handles. Nahal employs the internal monologue to describe Gandhi's historic march to Dandi. As Jeremy Hawthorn observes: "An internal monologue necessarily implies the use of *language*, and if an individual is 'talking to himself or herself' then that in turn presupposes a certain amount of consciousness of what is going on in that person's mind."[11] During the march Gandhi says:

> I celebrate and sing of India, I sing of its winds, rivers, trees, temples. . . . I must move on, I have to march 240 miles and reach Dandi, the whole world is watching me. (210)

Here, Gandhi is talking to himself, which, in turn, presupposes an awareness of the thought processes. The flow of thought is not only smooth but also rational. Each succeeding thought is a logical outcome of the previous one. Nahal uses flashback technique to narrate Raja Vishal Chand's death.

Coming to his stylistic devices, Nahal writes very long sentences. A single sentence, describing Gandhi's epoch-making march to Gandhi, spreads over forty-two pages. (175-216) It accomplishes "a nuclear fusion of time, place, character, mood, atmosphere, sensibility, dialectics, action, reaction, failure, fulfilment."[12] Later, to describe Kusum who is bracing herself to protest against the racial arrogance of the British, Nahal writes a sentence containing sixty-seven lines. ((276-278)

Nahal's manner of picturing life is almost untouched by idealism or romanticism. Consequently, *The Salt of Life* abounds in realistic detail. He describes Gandhi's early release from prison in 1942 on health grounds, his epoch-making march to Dandi, the tremendous response to Salt Satyagraha, terrorist activities indulged in by the revolutionary groups, discrimination of the Eurasians by the powers that be, the growing fears of the colonizer about Gandhi "acquiring an increasingly greater hold" on his countrymen, and escape of Subhas Bose to Russia.

Nahal gives a graphic account of the awakening among women brought about by Gandhi and their active participation in the liberation movement. The novelist's description of the festival of Mahalakshmi at Trivandrum and Raja Vishal Chand's pilgrimage to Gompah and Mount Kailash throw light on Indian way of life. Nahal shows how India's struggle for freedom results in the disintegration of families, forcing them to seek new identity. In the late 30s, in spite of Gandhi's best efforts to forge unity among the Hindus and Muslims, the latter view one another with suspicion. Nahal illustrates this by narrating how an accident involving Rai Bahadur's car and a bus is given a communal colouring and how both the Muslims and Hindus go on rampage without waiting to know the facts. As a result,

> The army at last was called out and peace restored in Amritsar but not until there were further firings in the city and twenty people had died in the riots, many more injured and many more stores burned down and looted. (456)

Nahal's repetition of the word "temper" while describing the temper of the Salt Satyagraha is indeed apt. "The temper of the present moment, its pace, its rhythm, its momentum was different. It was a faster temper. It was a bolder temper. It was a threatening temper." (263)

Chaman Nahal's use of language is noteworthy especially for its diction. His choice of words to describe Kusum's recollection of the sad and trying days of her life with Sunil is indeed remarkable. Nahal writes:

> Kusum went back repeatedly to the *Ramayana* and the *Mahabharata*, read those legends over and over again, settling in the end on the discourse of Krishna in the *Gita*, which was not an exhortation for murder, but an exhortation to withstand murder, to meet murder with murder if it came to that, but first to meet it with gentility, with peace and love, with affirmation, by silently doing one's duty, by silently following one's destiny. (35-36)

The words have a rhythm of their own, compelling our attention to them. Similarly, Nahal's description of love between Alan Cutlass, a British army officer and Ginger is nothing but a rhapsody on love. Alan with his taste for poetry, with Ginger, the woman he loves beside him and mist surrounding them, goes into raptures. Nature seems to partake of their joy. The mist that rejuvenates, when inhaled "wandered the hills in her own right, a clear, refined, gently perfumed mass of wafting air. . . . The mist having bathed them, moved ahead at a leap, taking swift strides." (476)

Each character in the novel speaks his or her own kind of language. That helps the novelist in giving a distinct touch to each character. To cite but a few examples, the toy maker, who rescues the young Abha at the festival of Mahalakshmi at Trivandrum, speaks broken sentences. This is natural keeping in view his poor knowledge of the language. He says: "Four children, wife dead recently . . . no money in toys. . . . Starving, amma." (120)

Similarly, Ginger's Welsh accent lends her a distinct touch. When Ginger speaks the 'lls' correctly in the word 'Llanferres' and brings out 'Khla' sound, Alan immediately tells her that she grew up in North Wales. Another instance of Nahal's intelligent use of language is naming of Raja Vishal Chand's princely state as Lambini, which has semantic resemblance to Lumbini, the birth place of the Buddha. Yet another instance of interesting feature of the novelist's language is the use of proverbs. For instance, while describing the women who are milking cows, Nahal cites the following proverb: "They say a a horse knows his rider by instinct. So does a cow her milker." (124)

Unlike Jonathan Swift, Chaman Nahal laughs with his characters. As a result, *The Gandhi Quartet* pervades with gentle humour. For instance, when Matthew Craig asks Gandhi why the latter held talks with Lord Irwin at night only, Gandhi replies: "I met Irwin at night because the Englishmen can think better then than during the heat of the day." (343)

The irrepressible priest, John Tree's christening of Indians after Indian seasons and household items provokes our mirth. Some of the names given by him are Henry Canal and Sally Monsoon. (312) When the government issues too many ordinances to stifle the movement for self-rule, Gandhi jocularly observes that Indians have now a very large number of laws to break and to offer satyagraha.

Along with gentle humour, irony of situation also forms part of Nahal's stylistic devices. John Tree believing the words of Joseph Daniel and his companion that their stranded van contains supplies to the church in Ugoki, helps them by pushing the van into the church. He is happy because "he could add one more item of grace to his day" and wishes them good luck. But the van contains kerosene and explosives and Joseph Daniel and his companion set the church on fire with them.

Perhaps, the most innovative of Nahal's stylistic devices is the introduction of the play "God or Gandhi" in the novel. Nahal seems to have been inspired by Gandhi's appreciation of the play, "Prahlada," performed in his presence in 1915:

> Mahatma Gandhi attended the Provincial Conference held at Nellore in 1915. On that occasion, the then District Collector, Sri Ramachandra Rao arranged the staging of the play, 'Prahlada.' Gandhi was so impressed by the performance of the artists that he broke his vow of silence, which he observes on Mondays, and complimented the artists. He then addressed and gave message to the people.[13]

Gandhi keenly watches the play staged by Percy Wand, Jennifer Wand, John Tree and Carol Schnicke in his ashram. He is so impressed by the show that he requests Carol Schnicke to repeat the performance each evening for a week. He realizes that the ultimate remedy for their sufferings in the imperialistic rule lies in salt only in that they must endure "ceaseless suffering" till they succeed in edging out the repressive regime from India and gain independence.

Nahal makes a telling use of the literary device of contrast in the novel. The British say that they are in India to "enforce civilized laws. . . . We are here to introduce democratic institutions." (322-23) But the same British, instead of honouring the Gandhi-Irwin Pact, start persecuting "the peasants for siding with the Congress" and arm themselves with more and more ordinances to suppress the nationalist movement. They are eager to convert as many Indians as possible to Christianity. But they are not willing to "confer equal honours upon the Indian converts."

The juxtaposition of the happy married life of Kusum and Raja Vishal Chand and Viran Vati and Lala Dharam Das may be cited as another example of Nahal's effective use of the technique of contrast:

> If she were offered a choice between giving herself to Vishal Chand and to Gandhi, she knew what she would unflinchingly choose—a heresy though the choice might be. No, it was no heresy, it was a blessing, as ennobling as a union with a mythical God. (234)

On the other hand, Viran Vati, Kusum's mother, calls her husband, Lala Dharam Das, a "pig," a "monster." As she is always petulant, harsh, and hostile, he seeks pleasure from other women. By contrasting the happy married life of Kusum with that of Viran Vati, Nahal illustrates how genuine love brings one to unalloyed bliss.

Besides, there is an ideological conflict between non-violence and use of force represented by Gandhi and Subhas Bose. A close study of the novel reveals that conflict is heavily weighted against use of force. Subhas Bose depends on the help of Japan to drive the British out of India. We may say that it is an ill-conceived plan because one cannot depend on a third country for national liberation and that too on Japan which made no secret of its imperialistic ambitions by occupying China, Vietnam, Malaya, Singapore and Burma in the Second World War.

Thus, in *The Salt of Life*, Chaman Nahal succeeds exceedingly well in his attempt to show how Gandhi achieves resounding success in Salt Satyagraha by dint of his steadfast discipline, hard work, and, above all, his unparalleled capacity to carry the masses with him, thereby revealing how Gandhi's second mass movement has contributed greatly to the social emancipation of Indian women. Nahal displays his skill in creating living characters and in making good use of such literary devices as internal monologue and contrast. His diction and his penchant for writing long sentences compel our attention. Nahal's introduction of the play 'God or Gandhi,' adds a new dimension to his exquisite narrative technique. Furthermore, the novel demonstrates Nahal's remarkable skill in blending fact and fiction.

NOTES

1. Tara Chand, *History of the Freedom Movement in India* (1972; New Delhi: Govt. of India, Publications Division, 1992), Vol. 4, pp. 124-25.
2. Chaman Nahal, *The Salt of Life* (New Delhi: Allied, 1990). Vol. 2 of *The Gandhi Quartet* (1993), p. 107.
3. Bhabani Bhattacharya, *Mahatma Gandhi* (1977; New Delhi: Arnold Heinemann, 1982), p. 220.
4. B. Pattabhi Sitaramayya, "Gandhi in His many Aspects," *Mahatma Gandhi: Essays and Reflections on His Life and Work*, ed. S. Radhakrishnan (1956; Bombay: Jaico 1986), p. 176.
5. Louis Fischer, *The Life of Mahatma Gandhi* (1953; Bombay: Bharatiya Vidya Bhavan, 1959), Part II, p. 23.
6. Hiren Mukherjee, *The Gentle Colossus* (1964; Delhi: Oxford University Press, 1992), p. 30.
7. *Loc. cit.*
8. Satyavrata Ghosh, *Indian Struggle for Freedom* (Delhi: B.R., 1988), p. 58.
9. K.R. Srinivasa Iyengar, "The Gandhi Saga," review of *The Salt of Life*, *Indian Literature*, 34.5 (1991), p. 173.
10. Shakespeare, "Sonnet 116," *The Sonnets* (New York: The Signet Classics, 1964), p. 156.
11. Jeremy Hawthorn, *Studying the Novel: An Introduction* (New Delhi: Universal Book Stall, 1992), p. 43.
12. K.R. Srinivasa Iyengar, "The Gandhi Saga," p. 175.
13. Nelanuthala, "Golden Age of Plays: Nellore Region: 1900-1950," *Zaminryot*, 1 Sept. 1989, p. 80.

Give Yourself in Selfless Love: *The Triumph of the Tricolour*

While *The Salt of Life* deals with the historic Salt Satyagraha, *The Triumph of the Tricolour* looks back to the freedom movement during 1942-1946. The novel begins with the launching of the Quit India movement in 1942 and ends with the formation of the interim government in 1946, and Gandhi reminding the people of the need to remain non-violent, and to love one another so that they may live in peace and amity. During this period the young patriots are guided by Jayaprakash Narayan and the revolutionaries among them by Subhas Bose. The novel projects Gandhi, Subhas Bose, Jawaharlal Nehru, Jinnah and the young Jayaprakash Narayan at the macro-level and Vikram, Amit and Joseph Daniel at the micro-level. Though moved by the same desire of freeing India from the British rule, they adopt different methods to achieve freedom.

The novel begins with an account of Gandhi's concern for India. He realizes that it is time the Congress launched another mass movement on an unprecedented scale. His extensive tour of India makes him conclude that the Hindus and Muslims will eventually come to a settlement between themselves because nowhere people demanded separation. On 8 August 1942, at a special meeting of the All India Congress Committee, the members pass the epoch-making resolution asking the British to "Quit India."

Vallabhbhai Patel and some other members ask Gandhi about the means to be adopted to give effect to the resolution and about the place of revolutionaries in the freedom movement. They seek his permission to adopt their own methods to realize the dream of attaining self-rule for India. Gandhi tells them that in spite of his regard for the revolutionaries, he cannot sanction violence. However, they are "free to interpret non-violence the way they want it."

Undaunted by the arrests of Gandhi and other leaders, the nation as a whole takes up the challenging task. In the absence of Gandhi and other leaders, a group of fiery young leaders surface from nowhere and inspire the people with their boldness and with the war cry "Do or Die." There is violence at many places and there are many cases of destruction of government property, blowing up of railway tracks and disruption of communication services. In consequence, the government resorts to extreme measures like aerial bombarding of certain civil areas. After the victory of British in Europe, the government machinery becomes more and more ruthless and arrests almost all the leaders. Consequently, the Quit India movement slowly dies out, but not before thousands of freedom fighters have laid down their lives.

The government releases Gandhi, but it tries to hold him responsible for the violence that erupted. Gandhi is aware that the "August Struggle" is more violent than the earlier two mass movements. Still, in 1944, he refuses either to condemn those freedom fighters who adopted violent methods or to withdraw the movement. He decides to muster more support by convincing Jinnah to join in their efforts to strike at the British imperialists. But Jinnah remains obdurate in his demand for a separate state for the Muslims. The government releases Jawaharlal Nehru, Sardar Patel and other leaders in 1945 as part of their conciliatory moves. With the surrender of Japan, Subhas Bose's moves to overthrow the alien government in India from outside the country are completely checkmated. While Bose is on his way to Tokyo, his plane crashes, killing him.

The new Prime Minister of England, Clement Attlee, announces his intention to get out of India by sending the Cabinet Mission. Gandhi and Jinnah fail to convince each other on the two nation theory. On the recommendations of the Cabinet Mission, elections are held and the interim government is formed. But Gandhi, instead of attending the swearing in ceremony of

Jawaharlal Nehru as the head of the government, goes off to places that witnessed the worst ever communal clashes. Later, at the prayer meeting, Gandhi holds the majority community responsible for the destruction and killings in the name of religion.

When he denounces the Hindus for not giving themselves in selfless love, two Hindu youngmen call him a Hindu renegade and pelt him with stones. They declare that love and non-violence are nonsense. People who talked of them earlier, have got nowhere with them. Requesting Jawaharlal to let the youngmen go, the bleeding Gandhi says, "That's why, it has to be said again and again."

The political turbulence prevailing all over India provides an illuminating backdrop to the story of Thakur Shanti Nath's family. Gyan Thakur is the grandson of Shanti Nath and chief petty officer in the Indian Navy. While on board with his cousin and girl friend, he hears the news of the Quit India resolution. A minor incident makes him and other Indian petty officers rise in revolt and seize the ship which shows that the reverberations of Quit India movement are being felt everywhere in the country. But the government crushes the mutiny on the ship. Vikram, son of Kusum, another grandson of Shanti Nath, joins Joseph Daniel and other revolutionaries in their efforts to embarrass the unwanted government. They successfully hijack a train carrying the Italian POWs to Jammu. Amit, Vikram's younger brother, joins hands with the tribal leader Padamrai Kranti to neutralize the imperialist enemy. They kidnap British officials, keep them in villages along the Ganges, brainwash and torture them and then let them off. Though they do not kill the kidnapped officials, the torture proves worse than that. Kusum, Shanti Nath's daughter-in-law, after the death of her second husband, stays at Banaras helping the deserted women. Naval Thakur, the grandson of Shanti Nath and a follower of Subhas Bose, returns to India after the defeat of Japan in the war. Gunjan, Shanti Nath's daughter-in-law, is brutally murdered by Wayne Griffith, who is actually after Amit. Later, he commits two more murders in similar gruesome manner. Naval, son of Gunjan, and Amit succeed in bringing the murderer to book Vikram is repulsed by the pseudo-Gandhians and their dependence on money to win the elections. So he withdraws from the contest and joins Gandhi in his padayatra in the places ravaged by communal carnage.

The Triumph of the Tricolour is neatly structured. The novel is divided into three parts—"Defiance," "Constraints," and "Release." The first part reveals how people are no longer afraid of defying the government that does not have the sanction of the people to rule the country. A minor incident of discourtesy to his girl friend and cousin emboldens Gyan Thakur to defy the British officers and mutiny. While Vikram and Joseph Daniel defiantly divert the train carrying Italian POWs, regardless of the consequences, they are joined by a few ordinary men and some Sikh devotees. Chaudhri Barkat Ali along with others defies the government by taking part in the Quit India movement. Under the leadership of Abha and Vikram, the residents of Mohalla Ballimaran defiantly refuse to donate to the war fund. Everyone including children ask them to quit the mohalla, Delhi and finally India.

In the second part, the novelist narrates the restraints one faces because of various factors. It shows how one is not free to act according to one's will. The political climate of the country makes it difficult for Kusum to fulfil her promise of taking Amit to Gompah and build a memorial to her second husband, Raja Vishal Chand. Alluding to the many youngsters who have chosen to become revolutionaries in the cause of the nation, Kusum says: "they were all prisoners of their constraints, passing through twilight zones."[1]

Jinnah's insistence on the Congress agreeing to the formation of Pakistan imposes constraints on the negotiations between him and Gandhi. Amit tells his mother that because of the brutalities committed by the police on the tribals, he is constrained to join the latter and fight against the government. As Japan surrenders to the Allied forces, Subhas Bose is constrained to disband the Indian National Army. It breaks the heart of Darbara Singh and he commits suicide.

The third part is concerned with the winds of change sweeping all over the country. The Indian Magistrate, exhibiting exemplary integrity and intelligence, declares that Jalalu is not the murderer and releases him. Only when she finally realizes that

Bapu's way is the only way, Kusum finds a release from fear and she is at peace with herself. The British notice the clouds gathering over the Indian horizon and the storm about to break. So they expedite their plans to quit India. India is set firmly on the road to freedom when the interim government is formed in 1946 and the Tricolour ultimately triumphs.

Thus, a close study of the three parts of the novel which are organically linked with each other reveals how *The Triumph of the Tricolour* is a structural triumph. The first part gives rise to the second and the third part emanates from the second, whereby the novel acquires a sense of unity.

The novel seems to be episodic in structure inasmuch as there are six episodes which are used to illustrate and highlight the main threads of the novel. The first episode relates to the mutiny on the ship, *Lonavla*. Gyan Singh Thakur's exemplary service for twelve years in the Indian Navy helps him to become the first Indian chief petty officer. He celebrates it by holding a party on his ship, the *Lonavla*. He invites his girl friend, Gurinder Kaur, and his first cousin, Abha, on board the ship. The Indian sailors join them. After the party is over, Gurinder, Gyan and Abha unintentionally enter the officers' bar. The officers don't get up for the ladies.

This insignificant episode brings home to Gyan the prejudice, disdain and contempt the English have for Indians. He also recollects the news of Quit India resolution passed by the Congress which was broadcast on the radio a short while before. He feels that they have suffered "these bastards for far too long." He is angry with the British officers and at the same time confused also. Finally, he becomes panicky, takes his service revolver out and orders the officers to get up for the ladies. He declares it to be a mutiny and with the help of other Indian sailors takes the command of the ship. The news is flashed to other ships. But unfortunately, no other Indian ship joins them in the mutiny. Finally, they are overpowered by the loyal Gurkha troops and the British officers are freed. Gyan and nine others die in the snap fighting. All the ten sailors killed are tied to posts at the Gateway so that the people can see who is in command in India.

Gyan who has no specific political feelings and who has declared that he will not trade the rank he has earned for any spinning wheel or a sickle and a hammer, under the impact of the Quit India resolution works "esoteric ideas of national justice and women's dignity into his hurts" which are purely personal and local. He and his friends fit Gandhi's Quit India call to the British as well into "this grim montage.:" They appear to have reposed too much faith in the readiness of other Indian sailors in other Indian ships to join in. Nevertheless, the mutineers succeed in showing that the British imperialists cannot hold India unless they use force on a large scale.

The abortive revolt in the Indian fleet that took place on 18 February 1946 appears to have provided the necessary inspiration for Nahal to write this episode. He is the first Indian English novelist to fictionalize it.

The second episode is concerned with the hijacking of a whole train by Vikram and other revolutionaries. The government comes down with a heavy hand shortly after the Quit India resolution is adopted by the Congress and rounds up all the leaders. Then, the members of AICC who have gone underground adopt a novel method of protest that is believed to have been suggested by Jayaprakash Narayan: "The strategy was to engage the government in a series of events in which it could be tried out and exhausted; be it the municipality, the railway workshop or the university." (52)

The sweepers in many towns strike work and dump the dirt near the local municipal office and the students refuse to take their examinations: "The activists and the dissidents spilled out like the proverbial beans, in the hundreds, even in the thousands. The government tried rounding up the beans but a good number of them remained spilled and rolling—causing that endless confusion." (52)

Vikram and Darbara too decide to do their best to embarrass the government. Inspired by Kusum, who in 1930 had shaken the government by stopping the prestigious Frontier Mail at Wazirabad, they hijack a whole train carrying Italian POWs to Jammu. Ironically, it is Vikram who has been brought up by Gandhi that suggests this plan to the Himmat: "What irked the authorities was the ease with which the revolutionaries had carried off the bluff. It was more daring than a robbery, burglary or dacoity. . . . To save face, the government played down the event." (70)

Nahal is the first Indian English novelist to fictionalize the part played by the underground AICC, consisting of Socialists and radical Gandhians and Jayaprakash Narayan in "the August Struggle" or the Quit India movement.

The third episode deals with the refusal to contribute to war fund on the part of a majority of Indians. Lord Wavell, the Viceroy, is happy because the princes, the zamindars and the landlords contribute heavily to the war fund. They do it because they know it is a good investment which would bring huge returns subsequently. But Wavell is peeved because the majority of Indians belonging to the middle and poor sections of society refuse to fall in line with them. So he orders door-to-door fund raising campaign for the war. A senior British police or army officer, a couple of constables and a couple of Indian officials form a team. And many such teams are formed.

Captain Wayne Griffith leads one such team to a mohalla in Delhi. As soon as the door is opened in answer to the constable's knock, Griffith raises his cane to his cap in salute, greets and says in Hindustani: "Hum chanda ke liye aya hai" (we have come for donation). Thinking that he is asking for some one named Chanda, the woman in the house replies: "Chanda? There is no Chanda here, Huzoor!" They get the same reply at many places. At other places the residents ask: "Has that scoundrel been up to it again?" However, a few understand that Griffith has come to collect donations and they give whatever money they can out of fear. It is a different story when Griffith and his team enter Mohalla Ballimaran where the residents are Muslims. He is forewarned about "the volatile Muslim temper. The men—my, they were walking detonators. And the women—they were no less." (146)

When Griffith asks them 'chanda' for war, the women in turn ask him, "is there a war on?" The men add that there is cholera on and famine on and they do not know if there is "a war on too." So they refuse to give donations. Some shout "begone." They resent the daily visit of Griffith to their mohalla and declare it an incursion. They decide to put an end to it by protesting peacefully under the leadership of Abha, Vikram, and Julie. But before they act, the children from every lane gather near Griffith's team and shout "Quit our Mohalla." Their resentment makes them add the slogan "Quit Delhi." Unintentionally, they add one more slogan to the earlier ones and shout: "Quit Ballimaran. Quit Delhi. Quit India."

The Muslim official of his team cautions Griffith that the children are "Allah's little angels" and he should not touch them. So Griffith leaves the place crest-fallen and with a nil contribution. The episode throws light on the infectious nature of the struggle against imperialism which makes even children defy and cause discomfiture to the lackeys of the government.

The fourth episode gives a satirical account of unfounded claims over graves. As part of the elaborate preparations against the Japanese invasion of India, the government introduces blackout drills at night, mock dog fights over the towns and start building concrete air-raid shelters. At Sialkot, while they are digging near the Fort to build air-raid shelter, some mounds surface. Bibi Amarvati, Lala Kanshi Ram's landlady, claims, on the basis of a few old scrolls, that those mounds were the graves of her ancestors.

Sir Kenneth Ashby, a retired British ICS officer and incharge of civil defence of Sialkot, is for levelling up the mounds, "let the dead lie there" and complete the shelter there. Then, Bibi Amarvati protests in an abrasive manner. She says that the Fort was once the burial ground of their clan. She cites the legend that at one time the palace of Raja Salivahan, an uncle of the Pandavas of the Mahabharata, stood there. The Raja was the founder of Sialkot. Puran was his first wife's son and Rasalu was by his second wife. As a result of the palace intrigue, the second wife succeeds in placing her son Rasalu on the throne. Then Puran became the disciple of the great tantric and mystic, Bawa Gorakh Nath and ultimately became a monk who performed many miracles. People venerate him as Bawa Puran Bhagat. Bibi Amarvati adds that she is the direct descendant of Puran Bhagat. The authorities must stop digging up the graves of her ancestors and restore the land to her. She has dozens of scrolls to support her claim.

On her request, Lala Kanshi Ram goes through the scrolls. Some of them contain the usual rigmarole about who begot whom. A few of them, surprisingly, are about the 1857 mutiny and the four Bawas who died "in the great uproar" and laid to rest there.

The Muslims in the city, though they do not have any scrolls to substantiate their claims over the graves, assert that they are Muslim graves. The situation becomes tense with claims and counter claims and there is the danger of Hindu-Muslim riot breaking out. But in the end, they discover that they are neither the Muslim graves, nor the Hindu graves, but Christian graves, of the four Europeans killed in the 1857 mutiny.

As a tailpiece, Nahal says that Bibi Amarvati, who was vociferous in her claims, is illiterate and cannot read. Lala Kanshi Ram realizes, but only in the end, that the word 'Bawas' also refers to the white-skinned.

The fifth episode is about the gruesome murder of Gunjan, Meena Devi and Viney Devi by Wayne Griffith. Amit, Padamrai Kranti, Kapil Kranti and their tribal followers revolt against the government by abducting and making captives of many British officials. They confine the kidnapped officials in the remote villages along the Ganges. They torture, brainwash and then let the captives out. Wayne Griffith is one of the British officials who is tortured and later, released. Mentally deranged and demented, Griffith develops homicidal tendency. He is after Amit. As he fails to lay his hands on Amit, he murders Gunjan, Meena Devi and Viney Devi at Ajitha, Banaras and Delhi respectively.

Griffith strips the women of their clothes, strangles and then stabs them fifty-one times. Naval, Gunjan's son, notices some weird signs on her mother's body. Incidentally, no one else notices them.

After a few days, one Richard Vidal from Ajmer writes a letter to *The Sentinel* expressing his opinion that Gunjan's murder was the result of family squabbles over division of property. He also writes: "And what a murder, the murderer stabbing the victim senselessly and making weird signs on her body in her blood!" (351)

Naval and Amit read the letter and are surprised how someone living in Ajmer could come to know of the weird signs on Gunjan's body, which even the police failed to notice. They at once go to Ajmer and make enquiries about Richard Vidal. One day, they notice him at the post office collecting mail that has come in the name of Wayne Griffith. They realize that Richard Vidal is none other than Wayne Griffith. Later, they successfully redirect a parcel from *The Sentinel* addressed to Wayne Griffith to the apartment of Richard Vidal. Naturally, Griffith is startled at this. Later, Amit surreptitiously collects a few papers with 'Swastika' signs drawn by Richard Vidal. He compares them with 'Swastika' signs drawn by Griffith when in confinement. Now, Amit and Naval are doubly sure that Richard Vidal is none other than Wayne Griffith, the murderer of the three women. Later, Griffith admits to the crimes. In the process of bringing Griffith to book, Amit and Naval save Jalalu, an innocent tribal youth, who is falsely implicated in the case.

The episode of the three murders reveals that the historical novelist, Nahal, is also capable of writing a thriller. The manner in which the murders are committed, the clue the murderer leaves behind, the investigation and final unravelling of the mystery behind the murders and the identity of the murderer are really thrilling. The episode also serves as a satire on people who are eager to offer their advice unasked.

The sixth episode constitutes Kusum's encounter with the vultures. Kusum accompanies Gandhi, Nehru, Vikram and Gandhi's men to render help to the survivors of communal clashes at Hauz Khas monument. They find a number of dead bodies with none to perform the last rites. The vultures chase the few survivors away and begin to devour the dead bodies.

While Gandhi, Vikram and others go to meet the survivors hiding in some bushes, Kusum stays back at the monument. After a few minutes, she notices a few vultures silently pecking away at a woman's arm. As the sight turns her stomach, she utters an exclamation. The vultures lift their necks and bloody beaks and look at her. She shrieks as she sees a similar ghastly sight in the next courtyard. Now, the vultures rise from the carcasses and swoop on her. For some time she becomes panicky and shrieks and yells for help. But soon the calamity reminds her that she is not merely a woman but the "personification of power" and "the giver of life to others." She tries to chase them away with her 'dupatta' even while she shouts for help. She enters a small room with a window with a masonry screen fitted into it. The vultures with their "flesh smeared beaks" try to enter the room by pushing the screen. Horrified, Kusum screams for help. However. the vultures fail to push through the screen and fly away. Kusum notices this before she swoons. At this stage, Vikram enters the room.

Kusum, who is in a state of delirium, is immediately taken to a hospital in Delhi. Soon, she regains consciousness but begins to look at the sky and repeat the words "the vultures are all over," "No one is safe," and "you must act while there is time." Vikram, Abha and Gandhi sit by her. Then, she has a dream in which she sees a presence smiling gently and telling her that through selfless love no fear could ever come near and destroy her. The presence also asks her to approach others every time with pity, compassion and generosity. At this stage, Kusum wakes up. With serenity, she tells everyone that Bapu's way is the only way.

She is happy Vikram is going with Bapu on padayatra to the places ravaged by communal conflagration. She adds that she too will join them. She says in delight that the sky is blue and clear. It can easily be said that the presence which Kusum sees is Gandhi. It is he who tells not only Kusum but everyone that love, generosity, pity and compassion alone help us in removing mutual suspicion and hatred and ultimately, help the Hindus and Muslims live in fraternity.

Nahal metaphorically says that the suspicion and religious animosity are the ever-hungry vultures that have been devouring the much-needed unity among the Hindus and Muslims.

A close study of the six episodes described above reveals their importance in the novel. These episodes should not be viewed as a series of events forming digressions in the novel, but as parts of sequence. Each episode throws light on the main issues in the historical narrative. So they are not unnecessary intrusions but integral parts of the whole. However, the two episodes—rival claims over the graves and Gunjan's murder—may be said to be not as essential as the other episodes, viewed strictly from the narrative needs of the novel.

The ordered and organized sequence of events and actions in *The Triumph of the Tricolour* reveals Nahal's skill in constructing a well-knit plot. The plot is concerned with the Quit India call given by Gandhi, the subsequent arrest of Gandhi, Nehru and other leaders, the role of young revolutionaries like Vikram, Amit and Joseph Daniel in the Quit India movement during the absence of Gandhi.

Apart from many minor characters, Nahal introduces as many as thirteen major characters in *The Triumph of the Tricolour*. The noteworthy feature is that while portraying all these characters, he is realistic as ever.

A study of Nahal's portrayal of Gandhi reveals the latter's multi-faceted personality. Notable among Gandhi's qualities are his faith in the ultimate success of the non-violent struggle and his forgiveness. In spite of acknowledging the fact that the revolutionaries are also votaries of freedom, he refuses to sanction violence for achieving freedom. He asks Padamrai Kranti to suspend kidnapping, torturing and brainwashing of the British officials.

Nahal illustrates Gandhi's forgiveness by narrating how Gandhi is not angry with the Muslim League for not joining him against the British in 1942. He calls Jinnah "a son of India—an illustrious son." While he is returning to the Birla House after his talks with Jinnah, people shout "Mahatma Gandhi ki Jai." Gandhi immediately shouts back "Jinnah bhai ki jai." People pick up the cue and begin to shout "Gandhi bhai ki jai, Jinnah bhai ki jai."

Gandhi's indictment of the Hindus at the prayer meeting angers the Hindu fanatics. Two youths call Gandhi a Hindu renegade and hurl stones at him. Though bleeding, feeling dizzy and in immense pain, Gandhi asks Nehru to let them go.

Gandhi is so humble that he never feels his ego is hurt. He does not hesitate to own mistakes and admit failure. He agrees he is mistaken in thinking that backward India has ended with the untouchables. He feels sorry for having neglected the millions of tribals. When his valiant effort to make Jinnah realize the contradictions in his demand for Pakistan fails, he honestly accepts defeat at the hands of the Muslim theocrat.

Nahal highlights Gandhi's uncanny perception. Gandhi is aware that a nation does not mean a group of people living together. But "a group of people who were born together, who lived together, who grew up together, who died together." (209) The Hindus and Muslims of India are born together and have been living together. In these circumstances, Gandhi is shocked to hear Jinnah say that the Muslims of India belong to a separate nation. He tells Jinnah that the partition of India will lead them nowhere.

Soon after the formation of the interim government, Nehru, Sardar Patel and other leaders happily declare that the Tricolour has triumphed. But Gandhi stuns everyone by saying that in India where the people are divided on race, religion, caste, status, language and regionalism, the Tricolour will never triumph.

Gandhi could well perceive the success of non-violent struggle in making the British quit India. But the failure of the revolutionaries and of Bose's Forward Bloc to arouse enough enthusiasm to start an anti-British mass movement go to prove that they lacked perception.

Nahal also throws light on Gandhi's typical acumen to twist everything in his favour. When the loyalists join Sir Kenneth Ashby in declaring that the British in India love India and they are patrons of India, Gandhi says that "he was happy the British in India at last saw where they belonged. Yet if they truly believed what they said, that they too were Indians, then they should be fighting Whitehall for India's independence. They should en masse join the Congress." (116)

After blessing the newly married Vikram and Julie from the prison, Gandhi adds: "now there would be two of you to fight for India. Yes, indeed, he expected Julie to join him in the fight." (122)

Nahal throws ample light on Gandhi's concern for the people. Gandhi is sad because even after two mass movements, India remains a slave nation "which couldn't raise its head in its own right. It had no national flag which could flutter alongside the flags of other nations; it had no national anthem which could be sung alongside theirs." (13) He realizes that the time has come for the Congress to launch the third mass movement. Its demand should be: "the British must quit. Leave India to Indians to make of it what they would. There would be no other terms and conditions of the new Congress movement. The British must leave, retire, go, vanish, disappear, pass out, pass away." (14)

As soon as Gandhi realizes that he cannot stop the vivisection of India, he turns "his thoughts to the major problems the country would have to face. He, therefore, decides to devote all his energy to minimise the evil effects of the decision, that is, to bring about communal harmony."[2] However, we cannot deny that Gandhi has many critics, Kasturbai being one of them. But it is because of their failure to understand his enigmatic personality that they criticize him.

After Gandhi, it is Jawaharlal Nehru who plays an important role in Indian struggle for freedom. Jawaharlal Nehru is Gandhi's discovery. He enjoys Gandhi's confidence. Gandhi many a time asks him to solve for him some of the puzzling issues. Gandhi takes Nehru before the victims of communal flare up and tells them the new government will protect them. Nehru promptly assures them of every help.

But Nehru's regard for Gandhi pushes him into a dilemma. Gandhi forbids the use of force to stop the savagery of the fanatics and tells that "love alone could override savagery." Yet, he leaves it to Nehru to decide whether to use force or not to quell the riots and restore peace. Nehru, who is always in a hurry to do things, feels that his hands are tied. He is annoyed and irritated. He tells Bapu: "I want to throw up—I don't think I can take this any more." (465)

Nehru is gentle but energetic, proud and assertive. A few minutes after assuming office, he receives a request from many soldiers of Delhi cantonment to attend Bapu's prayers. He instantly gives his permission. But Lord Wavell objects to it saying that soldiers must be kept away from politics. But Nehru refuses to yield saying that Gandhi does not represent the Congress Party alone but the entire nation.

If Gandhi symbolizes peaceful resistance to the British rule in India, Subhas Bose symbolizes armed resistance to the same. The attitude of Subhas Chandra Bose and the Indian National Army to the freedom struggle is best revealed in the words of Colonel Naranjan Singh Gill, a surviving member of the Indian National Army: "The non-violent struggle led by Mahatma Gandhi for attainment of all good objectives, was a light that mankind has to accept some day if humanity is to survive. Unfortunately, that stage in human history has not arrived yet. So, violence cannot be discarded for the achievement of just aims. Thus came the I.N.A. as a logical support to the efforts of the people of India to achieve Indian Independence."[3]

Subhas Bose's faith in the success of armed resistance to the government in India remains firm as a rock till his tragic death in an air crash. Even the defeat and surrender of Japan in the Second World War fails to extinguish that flame of faith. The Japanese not only badly let down but ask him to surrender. As a true soldier, patriot and one with immense faith in his followers and in his capabilities, he refuses to do it. He wants to lie low somewhere and launch an attack against India at the appropriate time. He tells his troops to disperse or "surrender as a temporary expedience. Spiritually they would keep themselves in readiness for his call. And when that call came, they would gather near him again." (300) But while he is on his way to Tokyo, he is killed in an air crash.

Nahal narrates how, in spite of his failure to realize the goal of driving the British out of India, Bose remains one of the inspiring leaders of India, whose sacrifice is no less than the other leaders:

> For years he had been pushing himself from one exile to another, driven only by one urge—to free India. And the goal eventually was almost in sight. He had taught his men to raise their hands high, and shout loud and clear, 'Jai Hind,' 'Glory to India.' He had reports that back in India these two words had been more readily adopted by

> the people than anything Gandhi might have churned out in thirty years. (293)

He has to stay away from his wife, Tanya and never had any opportunity to see their daughter. The Naval Mutiny at Bombay in February 1946 is the direct result of the I.N.A. trials. It makes the British realize that the Indian soldier is not merely a mercenary but one who is ready to die for the sake of his motherland. They also realize that they can no longer rely on the Indian army as their main base of power, which realization hastens their departure from India. The crowning achievement of Bose's I.N.A. is that its members set a very good example of communal harmony and comradeship.

While Gandhi declares that "through realization of freedom of India I hope to realize and carry on the mission of brotherhood of man,"[4] Jinnah insists on the division of one people into two different nations for personal gains on religious lines. It is interesting to note that in the beginning Jinnah was a staunch supporter of the Congress and a nationalist. He has a very high regard for Tilak. Once Justice Davar sentenced Tilak to six years' rigorous imprisonment and immediately, the government conferred a knighthood upon Davar. Jinnah felt that it is a shame on the nation. But the Bar Association, added insult to injury by deciding to honour Davar by hosting a dinner. Then, Jinnah wrote a scathing note: "the Bar should be ashamed to want to give a dinner to a judge who had obtained a knighthood by doing what the Government wanted, and by sending a great patriot to jail with a savage sentence."[5]

However, Jinnah detests Gandhi's talk of bullockcarts, loincloth and salt because he feels that they are anachronisms in the age of space. Still, Gandhi in appreciation of the young Jinnah's courage and spirit of nationalism confers the appellation of Quaid-e-Azam on him and he gracefully and proudly accepts it. As William Shirer rightly points out: "He [Jinnah] seemed to me at that time indifferent to his religion. He rarely worshipped at the mosque on Fridays. He had no compunction about breaking the laws of the prophet, including those that forbade the eating of pork, the drinking alcohol and marrying outside the faith."[6]

As if to prove once again that history is full of paradoxes, Jinnah, the most irreligious of men, becomes an unbending fanatic for a religiously ordered Islamic state and Gandhi, the most religious of Indians, fights till the end for secular India. Jinnah believes that the Congress is a party of Hindu communalists and the Muslim sentiment is "best represented by the Muslim League" of which he is the sole leader.

It is politics, not religious zeal that weans Jinnah away from secularist ideals. M.C. Chagla observes:

> Jinnah's transformation really began when it seemed to him that he was beginning to be considered as a man of little consequence—so much so that he could not even find a place in the Third Round Table Conference. Once he adopted the communal platform he drifted rapidly and came to a stop only when he reached the pinnacle to become the leader of the communal party that the Muslim League ultimately became.[7]

Jinnah adopts a very rigid stand in his talks with Gandhi. He insists that the plebiscite must be held first and then only should the British transfer power to the two nations. He refuses to be convinced of the contradictions in his arguments for a separate nation for the Muslims. He throws the entire blame for the backwardness of the Muslims on the Hindus and ignores the fact that government's economic policies are the main reason for it.

As Nahal has no intention of deifying any character, he also has no intention of blackening any character such as Jinnah. Jinnah sees Hindus, Muslims, Sikhs and Parsis going in the funeral procession of Salma Khan and the two workers. "They were literally marching shoulder to shoulder." Then he asks himself:

> Was Gandhi right, then? Was he, Mohammad Ali Jinnah, taking the Muslims on a needless collision course? What more would they get if they parted from India? . . . Would a Muslim after independence be happier with a non-identifiable Muslim or with an identifiable non-Muslim? (240-41)

But he once again looks at the motley crowd and tells himself that fellow feeling is not the same as identity and the Hindus and the Muslims have nothing in common between them really.

Gandhi and Nehru are also in a way responsible for making Jinnah believe that the Congress is biased towards the Hindus:

> While the Congress sharply demarcated itself from such bodies as the Hindu Mahasabha whose leader, V.D. Savarkar, spoke openly of India as "the abode of the Hindu Nation," it was a pity that Gandhi permitted a leading Congressman, K.M. Munshi, to resign and start his *Akhand Hindustan* movement. It was a pity also that the influence of Gandhi and Nehru was allowed to be exerted some time earlier in regard to the participation by important Congress leaders, including even such orthodox Muslims as Khan Abdul Gaffar Khan, in the ceremonial opening in Varanasi of a somewhat doubtfully secular *Bharatmata Mandir* (Temple of Mother India). On the temple's walls are engraved the alphabets of all Indian languages, but Urdu, which is entirely Indian, and particularly cherished by Muslims, is omitted because its script derives from abroad![8]

Through the portrayal of Vikram, Nahal reveals the aspiration and dilemma faced by the younger generation of freedom fighters in the 1940s. Vikram is honest and sincere in his desire to cure himself of his deficiencies. This sort of aspiration to strive for perfection under the impact of Gandhi is quite common to the youth of the time: "They set out in the pilgrimage of life with very laudable intentions. But when there is a conflict between what they themselves feel and know to be right and the inclination of the flesh, most of them abandon the right and pursue easier path of inclination."[9] However, this cannot be deemed as a failure on their part. It only shows how difficult it is to be a true follower of Gandhi. Vikram finds it impossible to keep some of the vows:

> He wore handspun, swadeshi, and he had no possessions,

> and he fasted until his ribs showed, yet he was not able to quell the hooded monster of his growing body. Came Julie Fogelson and he slumped into her arms and sobbed. (59)

He feels relieved when Julie tells him: "Don't worry, there can be celibacy through indulgence as well." (59) As a result, Julie becomes pregnant before marriage.

Nahal shows how the British are wrong in thinking that the incarceration of Gandhi and other leaders, immediately after the Quit India movement is launched, will make the youth feel rudderless. Their enthusiasm and spirit of sacrifice remains firm as ever. But in the absence of Gandhi, the Gandhian edicts come to be interpreted variously. Violence acquires a limited acceptability. Vikram too, saying that he will not kill anyone, takes part in violent activities. He is the author of the plan to divert the train carrying the Italian POWs to Jammu. When it is pointed out that while implementing the plan some pedestrians at the unmanned crossings might be killed, Vikram and his accomplices declare that "they only deserved that fate." Later, during the interrogation, he lies to Griffith about his part in the train hijacking episode. But these are only lapses on the part of a youngman who is leaderless. However, before long, the impact of Bapu's upbringing asserts itself. Vikram is aware that immediately after the elections, he will be rewarded with a ministership in the interim government. Still, he withdraws from the contest:

> I don't want this reward. You don't know how unhappy Bapu is these days. India is on the brink of being split into two countries and his heart bleeds at the thought of it. . . . He's planning to go on a padayatra, a village-to-village walk—to calm the communal frenzy. I won't fight the election. Instead I'll join him on his padayatra. (434-35)

He refuses even to work for the party or go to Delhi to work for Nehru but reiterates his decision to join Gandhi in his padayatra whether Julie joins him or not.

Vikram proves the relevance and efficacy of non-violent

way of protest at Mohalla Ballimaran. The residents of the mohalla are firm in not donating any thing to the war fund. The fund collection team is equally firm not to leave the place with a zero contribution. Then, Vikram and the residents offer satyagraha. As a result, the authorities are forced to turn tail and leave.

Amit, son of Kusum by Raja Vishal Chand, is presented as a foil to Vikram. Though he is the prince of Lambini, he is not interested in leading a luxurious life. He does not like the presence of the British in India. Though he is only eleven, he decides to revolt against the government by kidnapping the British officials. For this he takes the help of the tribal Chief Padamrai Kranti and his son, Kapil. They successfully abduct a few British officials. They torture and brainwash them:

> These Ferangis, the British, have scorched our country black and dry. Apparently, Subhas Bose has failed in Imphal. That Gandhi failed a long time ago—he is lying flat, even though the British have released him. (266)

When he learns that Vikram is involved in the hijacking of the train carrying the Italian POWs, he is happy that his brother is also embarrassing the unwanted government.

Amit has affection and regard for the elders. But he has no inhibitions and is too frank to spare anyone for their lapses. He is angry with Bapu for neglecting the tribals and for not involving them in the freedom struggle. When his mother questions him about his loyalty to her, without mincing words, he asks her about her loyalty to him. He smokes in the presence of the elders. He dislikes Gurinder and others for quarrelling over the division of property while Thakur Shanti Nath is on his death bed. As soon as he notices his grandfather struggling to breathe, he moves swiftly and saves him.

Nahal appears to endow Amit with clairvoyant foreknowledge that is "a secret perception, to which he alone had the key, a key he had come to have only accidentally, without volition, without a will on his own part." (78) But the truth is that Amit with his keen sense of observation and understanding is able to read others's thoughts.

Amit reveals his remarkable comprehension of the ways of the world when he says that there is a lot of humbug around him: "I put on a jacket and tie and I become a sahib. I put on khaddar, and I become a Gandhian." (82) He firmly believes that neither Gandhi's non-violence nor the Buddha's perpetual smile will help in ameliorating the sufferings of the people. So he requests Matthew Craig to spend his windfall money for the welfare of the tribals.

While Amit always looks for an opportunity to embarrass the alien government that has demoralized the country, Thakur Shanti Nath takes every opportunity to tell his children that freedom can be achieved through a dialogue with the British. So he expects his children not to oppose but serve the government and lead a secure life. He is under the illusion that an Englishman will allow an Indian to meet him on equal terms.

Thakur Shanti Nath is a relic of the bygone era who fails to take note of the sweeping changes that have been taking place in the country and society. So he feels himself to be an anachronistic before his grandchildren. However, he makes no attempt to catch up with them. He thinks that he is the most intelligent person and one who retains a "dignity superior to anything" that the youngsters possess. Though neither his children nor grandchildren obey him, he continues to have faith in the joint family system. We feel sorry for this presumptuous patriarch.

Nahal's portrayal of Lala Kanshi Ram is meant to serve as a satire on the loyalists and on people who consider themselves Know-Alls. Lala Kanshi Ram feels sorry for his countrymen because they are very simple-minded. He feels that "the stupidity of this land was beyond measure and he wondered what would have happened if intelligent men like him were not around!" (86) So he takes it upon his shoulders to explain to everyone about the intricacies of the preparations of the government to face any threat of invasion from the Japanese. He is proud of everything that is British. To him, even the air-raid sirens are part of the pageantry of the whitemen. Seeing people running helter-skelter soon after the sirens are sounded, he begins to laugh. How can he have fun if they are as intelligent as he is and stay indoors, feels Lala Kanshi Ram. He can wax eloquent even on moustaches and prove that Hitler's moustache is "a disgrace for all self-respecting persons." He tells his wife that at night a lit cigarette is visible as far as twenty miles and a sure target for the enemy pilot to attack.

Lala Kanshi Ram's unfounded faith in his intelligence makes him a megalomaniac. In the dispute over the digging of the graves to build air-raid shelter at the Fort, even though "the authorities had not sought his help, Lala Kanshi Ram felt it his bounden duty to intervene. How could he let his masters down in the hour of their peril!" (90) He declares that air-raid shelter must be built. This noted grain merchant of Sialkot feels that he

> had the divinity already in him, who already had some measure of the great God in him (he worried a little about the exact percentage), who had the divine in him in flesh and blood. (91)

While everyone is unhappy about the destruction being caused by the Second World War, he welcomes it saying, "why wouldn't they have a war going forever, or blackout forever, so that some discipline might descend on his unruly countrymen (saving himself)." (93)

Lala Kanshi Ram's adulation of the British borders on abject slavery. He declares that they are nothing if not logical:

> They moved, argued, lived, conducted themselves, strictly in accordance with a plan. They were logical even when they hanged a man or shot him dead; they had a doctor handy to certify the man was truly dead. (94)

In spite of his adulation of the British, Lala Kanshi Ram with a moan of regret admits that the freedom struggle is gaining momentum and the British may have to leave India. He is impressed by Gandhi but is not as committed to the freedom struggle as his friend, Chaudhri Barkat Ali. Presumptuous as he is, he decides to jump into the liberation movement only at the right time.

But alas! even the omniscient Lala Knashi Ram commits a few mistakes. He thinks the word 'Bawas' written in the scrolls refers to the monk Bawa Puran Bhagat and his descendants, whereas it actually refers to the white-skinned persons. Later, when he hears that one of the members of the cabinet mission is maintaining a "diary," he mistakes it for "dairy." He thinks that beef-eating has resulted in shortage of cows in England and so they want to import milk from India and "cut their costs down." He declares that the Hindu blood on the hands of Gandhi and the Muslim blood on the hands of Jinnah reveal the traces of the gypsy in them.

If Lala Kanshi Ram is abjectly slavish, Joseph Daniel is virulently anti-British. Joseph Daniel and the revolutionary outfit, Himmat, are presented as a foil to Gandhi and his non-violent struggle for freedom. After the attack on the Prince of Wales in 1922, some of the members of the Himmat are sentenced to death, some are deported to the Andamans and others leave the organization for good. Joseph Daniel escapes arrest and manages to keep "its torch alive and burning." Joseph Daniel, the violent revolutionary thinks that Gandhi is only a "white collar revolutionary." He says:

> Vande Mataram, fine. Vaishnava Janate, fine. Raghupati Raghava Raja Ram, fine. Oh, Mahatma, Sir, you don't know how innocuous and harmless the British regard you. Would they pamper you otherwise the way they do? (129)

But "the flaming words of Tilak and Gokhale" inspire him and he too declares that freedom is his birthright and it must be won either through labour or struggle or even force. He sacrifices everything for his cause. He loses all contact with his family, changes his address often, goes without food and the comforts of a happy home. Though he is only forty, the irregular living begins to take its toll. But it is his allegiance to the cause, true revolution, that keeps him alive. He proudly asks whether Gandhi has ever experienced such privations. He is bitter that Gandhi and the Congress have paid scant regard to the sacrifices of the revolutionaries.

The trio, Joseph Daniel, Naval Thakur, and Darbara Singh, believe that the call of the hour is to liquidate the enemy. For this, they pin their hopes on Subhas Bose who seeks the help of Japan to strike at the alien government in India. But the sudden turn of tide against Japan in the Second World War almost annihilates the revolutionary movement. The cold reception given to Subhas Bose by the Japanese and their conclusion that he is now a liability push Darbara Singh to commit suicide. Joseph Daniel and Dulari are killed in action. Ill-equipped as they are, they depend on an outside source for help. It reveals the inherent weakness of the movement led by Joseph Daniel. It is doomed to fail as in fact it does.

Nahal's delineation of Kusum is evidently based on Gandhi's conception of women's role in contemporary society: "Mohandas Karamchand Gandhi endorsed women's role outside the home in certain specific areas; he actively worked against the dominant image of woman as victim as the helpless creature to be subjugated." [10] A few days after the death of her second husband, Kusum overcomes her grief and decides to rehabilitate twenty destitute women. She is sorry she is not able to help more women: "You could wipe only as many tears and not all. Still one tear less was a help." (169) She encourages Abha to adopt a child though it is against the Islamic edicts. When they learn that the child, Gulbadan is deaf and dumb, Kusum exhorts Abha to "fight the fates" and make the child into "a symbol of defiance and daring." Kusum requests Abha to join her in raising "the flag of womanhood" high, if necessary, by defying convention and even God and usher in a new dawn in their lives.

Kusum reveals her insight when she says that the first priority of the liberators is to see that the forces unleashed by the Quit India resolution go forward even in the absence of Gandhi, Nehru and other leaders:

> The iron might never be as hot again and they had to strike at the anvil *now*. What did 'Do or Die,' the call Gandhi had given, otherwise mean? Did you go about it by the rule book? (188)

So she throws her weight behind the revolutionaries. The seven goddesses, Bhavani, Naina, Mansa, Vaishno, Kalika, Jwala, and Durga inspire her to become their sister and in her newly acquired power touch and uplift others: "she had truly taken on the role of Shakti. She had truly become the mother of them all." (189)

Kusum is ingenious. As there are too many khadi stores in Banaras selling handspun cotton cloth, she advises the women in her Savera Kunj to weave silk sarees and add a bit of colour to khaddar to attract more buyers.

If Kusum becomes a Shakti at times, she is no different from any other woman at other times. Amit's rudeness, belligerence and his remarks on Gandhi shock her. She begins to pity herself thinking that both her sons are neglecting her. She feels that even Gandhi would be of "no help to her right now." So she thinks of committing suicide. However, soon, she regains her composure and says: "The past is gone, and the present is in the process of becoming the past; only your future is all yours. Shape it the way you want it, dream upon it, fantasize on it, live for it." (123)

In spite of her long association with Gandhi, Kusum, like many others, fails to imbibe Gandhian ideology completely. Knowing fully well Gandhi's dislike of ostentation, she erects an imposing memorial to Raja Vishal Chand. When a few candidates exploit the name of Gandhi to garner votes by calling themselves "Banarsi Gandhi," "Amritsar Gandhi," she does not find fault with them. She says that what matters is that the Congress candidates must win the elections. Thus, they completely ignore Gandhi's dictum that means are more important than ends, even when he is alive.

But the violence that breaks in the opening months of 1946, makes Kusum realize that there is something precious in what Gandhi has been telling all these days: "Wasn't tenderness and love infinitely more durable than the slap on the face?" (467-68)

While many Congressmen are busy winning elections by hook or by crook so that they can climb the seat of power, Gandhi "old man of seventy-six, who should be resting in a quiet home, was still striving, still struggling, to dispel the gloom of fear. For Gandhi a slap for a slap was no answer." (468) She, along with Vikram joins Gandhi in his padayatra to restore communal harmony because she realizes that "Bapu's way is the only way."

The movement to liberate India from the clutches of the British imperialists results in the disintegration of many families forcing many seek new identity. The young Abha is one among them. Active involvement in the revolutionary activities and death sentence passed against him force Rakesh, Abha's father, to stay away from his wife and daughter. As a result, Shyama, Abha's mother marries Zahir Mustafa, and leaves her native place. Abha is forced to adapt herself to entirely different surroundings and people, which is not an easy thing for one so young as Abha. As a result, she feels lonely and becomes lachrymose. But after obtaining a degree in medicine, Abha makes an earnest effort to know who or what exactly she is. After some introspection, she decides to have nothing to do either with her Hindu mother or Muslim father or relatives or friends. She takes the train to Delhi, because

> the Muslim women in the walled city needed urgent medicaid. They wouldn't go to hospitals for inoculations, they wouldn't admit men doctors into their homes; they would rather die of cholera than make compromises with their faith. (126)

As days pass, she succeeds in setting their houses in order and in doing so, she sets "her own house in order as well. The house of her faith, her identity. The scales had tipped only imperceptibly. But she knew where she belonged." (126-27)

Soon, her petulance and irrationality give place to forgiveness and confidence to state her views freely. She apologizes to Kusum for blaming her for her father's death. Later, she tells everyone in the mohalla not to offer anything to the war-fund. She asks them to slam the door in the face of the fund collection team because the government is utterly callous to the people who are victims of cholera and famine.

Abha, though young, realizes that the source of true love is God. The thought of the Almighty makes her "feel so clear, so pure" and God becomes her mainstay. As a result she decides to remain a spinster and serve the people with love. When she finds an abandoned female child, she wants to adopt her and bring her up. But the Islamic edicts refuse sanction for such an adoption, leaving her in a fix. However, she does not like to leave the child, "a creation of Allah," to be neglected. But Kusum's words, "Women should learn to live for themselves!" give her courage and she declares:

> I'll stay a Muslim and bring up this child as Muslim too, Kusum mami encourages me in this, assert from where you are, don't prevaricate, shout out what it means to be a woman and insist on your freedom, your independence. (456)

She names the child Gulbadan and soon experiences how great it is to be a mother. But gloom descends on her, when she learns that the child is stone deaf. She fails to understand why God has punished her, in this way, though she has lived an upright life. But earlier her faith in Allah had given her strength to face boldly the taunts and the ridicules her squint invited. Now, she feels she is going through hell again. But again, Kusum's words of encouragement drive the gloom out of her and "a strange resolve" surfaces in her. She says that she will "fight the fates as well."

Abha, the personification of love, fails to comprehend the ways of the people around her. She is shocked to see the carnage going on in the name of religion. While some people are killing one another in the name of their God, others are contesting the elections. Those who have been working only for their personal gains now call themselves freedom fighters and freely use the name of Gandhi to win the elections. Seeing the Congress Tricolour fluttering everywhere after the elections, Abha does not feel elated because no one is quite clear of the kind of free India people would want.

Glady Mitchell, the retired Eurasian nurse, is a typical example of Anglo-Indians who are neither here nor there. Her contempt for the Indian Christians stands in the way of her marrying one of them. At the same time, the Englishmen's racial prejudice makes it impossible for her to find an Englishman who is willing to marry her. She suffers from inferiority complex and pretends to be a pure-bred Englishwoman, who has been patiently waiting for an Englishman to marry her.

But she finds it very difficult to control her carnal desires till she gets married. She sleeps with Rakesh at Amritsar. When the young postman asks her for a glass of water, she knows it is a ruse to touch her. Then, she smiles and tells herself: "But, dear boy, thirsts such as yours can't be quenched by water alone. You must proceed from step one to step two." (396)

Glady at last finds an Englishman who promises to marry her and take her to England. He is Wayne Griffith, a British army officer, now her tenant. She readily becomes his mistress. But her dream of marrying an Englishman is shattered when Griffith is found to be the maniac who has brutally murdered three women.

Matthew Craig, an American teacher from Kentucky, represents the group of Westerners who are rich but not happy and who come to India to find peace in Hinduism. He even writes a book on Hinduism and Christianity. He protests that Hinduism denies entry to non-Hindus into temples, neglects the untouchables and women. In spite of these anomalies, Hinduism offers a healing touch to people, which even lots of money cannot do. Kusum, a Hindu, says that most of Hinduism is just a gimmick. Then, he asks her whether the Ganges is a gimmick. If it is so, millions of people would not be going there.

As a teacher in the Lambini Public School, he closely observes Amit. When he tells Kusum that Amit misses her and it is better she keeps him with her, he is only arraigning her for neglecting her duty as a mother. He gives away his wealth, inherited from Celia Ashby, to the YMCA to look after the tribals and to Kusum to build a home for the aged. He believes in non-possession. So he wants to mismanage all his recently inherited wealth as quickly as possible so that he can lead a simple life. He is a typical discontented youth from the West who seeks refuge in the religious India.

As regards the narrative technique of *The Triumph of the Tricolour*, Chaman Nahal employs the third person point of view. However, to describe Abha's dilemma over adopting a child, objections to it from the religious heads and her final resolve to adopt the child by defying the whole world, if necessary, Nahal adopts first person narrative by making use of Abha's diary. He also adopts the epistolary form, which has received very little attention from the Indian English novelists. He is aware of "the effect of persons revealing themselves without external analysis or description, and being seen from more than one angle; the reader thereby arrives at an intimate knowledge of both characters and events, built up with the minute accuracy of a Dutch painting."[11] Nahal makes an effective use of this device to reveal the reactions and views of different people to the ghastly murder of Gunjan and two other women.

Nahal makes a sustained effort to ensure that factual details of both the social and political life of the 1940 are faithfully presented in *The Triumph of the Tricolour*. He narrates the Quit India resolution passed on August 8, 1942, the arrests of all the prominent leaders the next day, Jayaprakash Narayan providing the leadership in the absence of Gandhi, the successful efforts of the freedom fighters in embarrassing and neutralizing the enemy of the nationalist movement, the ruthless repression that follows, disbanding of the Indian National Army by Subhas Bose soon after Japan surrenders, Gandhi and Jinnah's failure to convince each other over the bifurcation of the country, the Cabinet Mission's visit, the holding of elections and the formation of the interim government under the leadership of Jawaharlal Nehru in 1946 and the internecine quarrels between the Hindus and Muslims—these are the principal historical incidents realistically presented in the novel.

The society in the novel is portrayed realistically. Women come out openly and fearlessly and take part in independence movement. They make their own assertions and try to seek their identity. Abha's quest for identity ends when she decides to serve Muslim women as a doctor and asserts herself by adopting a child though it is against Islamic edicts. Salma Khan leads the mill workers from the front and dies while fighting for their welfare. Another instance of social realism is the description of the Ganges and the holy city of Banaras. The former is called the holy Ganges by the devotees and the unholy Ganges by the ecologists. Nonetheless, it attracts millions of devotees throughout the year. People have so much faith in its holiness that its attraction is described as "infectious." Yet another instance of social realism is the description of the effect of industrialization over the rural India. The village, Ajita, is transformed into a town: "Ajita, as it turned out, was a living rejection of all that Gandhiji stood for in terms of economy and development." (327)

Nahal portrays realistically what people do in almost all Hindu families when one of them is on death-bed. While the old and seriously sick Thakur Shanti Nath wants to get well, his kith and kin keep the oil and wick and the Ganges water ready.

Chaman Nahal's use of language renders the narration dignified and moving. Darbara Singh, after successfully resisting the attempts of a few Congress volunteers to shout him down, speaks about the sacrifices made by the revolutionaries. He says:

> I may or may not be a Congressman—though I *am* wearing khaddar. . . . Yet my voice is not the voice of a foe—I'm as ardent a votary of freedom as any. Many of the Congress delegates here have spent spells in jail. So have you, Mahatmaji—four precious years of your life, off and on. But so have others who may not be subscribing to the Congress creed—and longer periods than you can imagine. There are people in this audience who have lived in dungeons of the British for *twenty year—twenty-five years*. Can we, with any honesty, disregard their sacrifices or write them off casually? (22)

Nahal's repetition of words, indeed, creates a marvellous effect:

> At Churchgate one could continue counting heads from morning till evening. Heads upon heads upon heads. Legs

> upon legs upon legs. Feet upon feet upon feet. Shoes upon shoes upon shoes. (218)

Nahal lends a distinct touch to the character of Sir Charles Tenor by making him divide certain words into as many syllables as he likes. He divides the word family into *fa-mi-ly*, genius into *ge-nius*, unbeatable into *un-bea-table*, and brilliant into *bril-liant.*

The novel shows how Nahal has a fascination for writing long sentences. For instance, while describing the relationship between Joseph Daniel and Dulari, Nahal writes a pretty long sentence containing sixty-eight lines. (131-33)

Another feature of Nahal's style is the occasional use of too many adjectives for the sake of emphasis. Lala Kanshi Ram, while giving his estimate of his countrymen, says: "The Indians are playful creatures, worshipful, devotional, emotional, blissful, childlike, idolatrous." (109)

As part of his stylistic devices, Nahal employs various figures of speech. For instance, he employs onomatopoeia to present a realistic picture of the movement of the train:

> They heard a train chug-chugging, chug-chugging on that deserted line which had never been ever used at night, with not a hoot, with not a whistle, but chug-chugging-chug-chugging-chug-chugging ahead at increasing speed. (67)

When Vikram learns that his English wife, Julie, has decided to stay back in India and the latter is under stress because she must stay in an alien country for his sake, he compares her to Ruth of Keats' "Ode to a Nightingale: "Oh, a Ruth—is that what she is! A Ruth amidst alien corn!" (436)

Wayne Griffith learns from the tourist guide that there are three paths to 'Nirvana,' nine hundred and ninety ways of kissing a woman's lips, and fourteen ways of tickling a woman. These statements baffle him and as a result he goes mad. Here is a fine instance of a hyperbole of the Hindu propensity for divisions and sub-divisions.

Nahal's genial humour makes us laugh with and not at the characters. Wavell believes that the uncrowned king of India, Mahatma Gandhi, and the Indians are only bunch of idlers and there is no threat to the Raj from them. He sends a cable to that extent to Churchill. But the cable reads: "Idlers all stop including king stop crown ours." (143)

Punning on the word 'chanda' Nahal creates a beautiful incident where the Indians discomfit the team that goes to collect war fund. When the members of the team say in Hindustani that they have come for 'chanda' (donation), the people shut the door on their face saying that there is no Chanda (a person called Chanda).

Nahal employs irony to reveal how things have changed for the worse even when Gandhi is alive. In 1931 Gandhi wrote: "Having flung aside the sword, there is nothing except the cup of love which I can offer to those who oppose me. It is by offering that cup that I expect to draw them close to me."[12] It is ironical to note that in 1946, Jawaharlal Nehru is afraid that some communalists might attack Gandhi. So he tells Bapu: "Anyone can storm your hut, anyone can harm you, Bapu, he muttered." (461)

Nahal is probably under the influence of the pre-Raphaelites while describing the physical features and appearance of almost all the characters. To describe Gandhi at the prayer meeting, Nahal writes as many as twenty lines and writes another ten lines to describe the appearance of Vikṛam, thereby making us feel that those characters virtually stand before us.

The dominating symbol of the novel is the Congress flag, the flag which represents the nationalist movement. Soon after the elections are over and even before the interim government is formed, the Tricolour begins to flutter atop every building, thus indicating victory to the freedom fighters.

The presence which Kusum sees in her dream stands for the apostle of peace, Gandhi, and the vultures symbolize jealousy, hatred, selfishness and the divisive forces.

It may be pointed out that there is polarity of opinion among the freedom fighters. Gandhi believes that there is no alternative to non-violent struggle. Subhas Bose, Joseph Daniel,

Amit and Gyan Thakur believe that violent methods alone will drive the British away from the country.

As soon as the people realize that the British are going to quit India, many of them, including Abha and Julie, come to believe firmly that Gandhi is no longer relevant. But Kusum, in the end, realizes that Gandhi's way is the only way.

Nahal employs the method of contrast with telling effect in the novel. Sardar Bhajan Singh is a rich hosiery merchant. He is philanthropic and his motto is: "be good to workers." But Sardar Nirmal Singh asserts that "factories are run on the profit motive." Salma Khan, a member of the Himmat, dies while fearlessly fighting to protect the interests of the workers. But Gunjan, for the sake of grabbing a major share in the property, forms an illicit relationship with Kanti Nath. Kenneth Ashby is for the perpetuation of the British Raj in India and he does not like Gandhi. Still, as a result of his prolonged stay and service in India, he resolves to stay on even after the country becomes independent. Wayne Griffith, however, finds India too baffling and decides to purge India of Indians and Eurasians so that the British can stay here forever. To Abha, freedom means having nothing to do either with her mother or with any of her relatives so that she can serve the women as a doctor. Gurinder's sense of freedom and liberty make her remove her blouse, spread her naked flesh open before Gyan and run the length of the deck on the *Lonavla.* While Abha remains firm in her resolve not to marry, so that she can render medical aid without any encumbrances, Gurinder, after Gyan's death, sleeps with Naval and is unhappy with Nirmal Singh for not making overtures to her.

Thus, Chaman Nahal in *The Triumph of the Tricolour* successfully reconstructs India's struggle for freedom during 1942 and 1946. His attention to detail, the characaters, the historical accuracy and the tenor of Indian life is superb. He is the first Indian English novelist to fictionalize the significant, but often ignored, role of the young revolutionaries who were inspired by Jayaprakash Narayan in the Quit India movement. His introduction of as many as six episodes and his use of diary and epistles as part of the narrative in first person make the novel highly gripping. Nahal reveals his skill as a historical novelist by making the historical and fictional characters interact in a convincing manner.

NOTES

1. Chaman Nahal, *The Triumph of the Tricolour*, vol. 3 of *The Gandhi Quartet* (New Delhi: Allied, 1993), p. 198.
2. J.B. Kripalani, *Gandhi: His Life and Thought* (1970; New Delhi: Govt. of India, Publications Division, 1991), p. 290.
3. Colonel Naranjan Singh Gill, *Story of the I.N.A.* (New Delhi: Govt. of India, Publications Division, 1985), p. 68.
4. M.K. Gandhi, *Young India*, 4 April 1929.
5. M.C. Chagla, *Roses in December* (1973; Bombay: Bharatiya Vidya Bhavan, 1978), p. 15.
6. William Shirer, "Gandhi's Dream, Jinnah's Design," *Sunday Chronicle*, 30 Jan. 1994, p. 3.
7. M.C. Chagla, pp. 79-80.
8. Hiren Mukerjee, *The Gentle Colossus* (1986; Delhi: OUP, 1992), p. 100.
9. Khasa Subba Rau, "Gandhi, the Mahatma," *Footfalls*, ed. Harindranath Chattopadhyaya (Hyderabad: Writers' Anvil, 1976), p. 72.
10. Malavika Karlekar, "The Relevance of Mohandas Karamchand Gandhi: A Contemporary Perspective," *Indian Journal of Gender Studies*, 2.1 (1995), p. 62.
11. Leslie Stephen's words as quoted by Kenneth Graham in his *English Criticism of the Novel*: 1865-1900 (London: OUP, 1967), p. 133.
12. M.K. Gandhi, *Young India*, 2 April 1931, p. 54.

A Wiped Out Dream: *Azadi*

While *The Triumph of the Tricolour* narrates the Quit India movement and events leading to the formation of the interim government in 1946, Chaman Nahal's *Azadi*, which forms the fourth volume of *The Gandhi Quartet*, deals with the partition of the subcontinent into India and Pakistan. The novel presents how man is a victim of forces of history and how religion, at times, arouses mind numbing beastiality. The novel also shows how 'azadi' or freedom India wins fizzles out to be a "false dawn of freedom" or "a wiped out dream."

Though *Azadi* narrates the sorrowful tale of five families, the fictional focus is on Lala Kanshi Ram's family. Lala Kanshi Ram, the protagonist, is a well-established and complacent grain merchant in Sialkot in West Punjab. When he hears Nehru on the radio asking the people to be ready for partition in case there is no alternative, he fails to understand the need for the division of the country. He wonders whether bifurcation of a vast country like India is possible "at such short notice." Even after the announcement pertaining to the partition is made over the radio, he hopes that at least for economic reasons, he will be allowed to stay in Sialkot, which is now a part of Pakistan.

However, the looting, the killings and the fires frighten and demoralize the Hindus and expose the vulnerability of the minority community. As a result, Lala Kanshi Ram, his wife Prabha Rani, his son Arun, and their neighbours take shelter in the refugee camp. The bifurcation of the country forces separation on the young lovers, Arun and Nur, the daughter of Chaudhri Barkat Ali. Lala Kanshi Ram's cup of woe is full when he receives the news of the death of his daughter Madhu and her husband at the hands of Muslims. It becomes the final straw which shatters his fond hope of going back to Sialkot. He and the members of his family join the foot convoy to India in their search of identity.

From Sialkot it is a long, difficult, arduous and terror-filled march to Dera Baba Nanak. In spite of an armed escort, the convoy witnesses incessant attacks, killings and abduction of women by Muslims. At a few places, they become silent spectators of the parading of naked Hindu women. Arun kills Captain Rahmat-Ullah Khan for raping Sunanda. He fails to trace Chandni with whom he is in love, and it shatters his dream of leading a happy life.

Soon after setting foot on the Indian soil, Lala Kanshi Ram observes the mutilation, murder, rape and parading of naked Muslim women. He is dumbfounded to note Hindus equally frenzied. Finally, he reaches Delhi with Prabha Rani, Arun, Bibi Amarvati, Sunanda and her children. Later, he hears the sad news of the assassination of Gandhi. Lala Kanshi Ram opens a small grocery-shop and Sunanda buys an old sewing machine and they start their lives afresh.

The division of the plot as well as the narrative sequence clearly brings out Nahal's skill in architectonics. The novel is divided into three parts—"The Lull," "The Storm" and, "The Aftermath." Each one of these titles carries tremendous psychological significance. The first part "The Lull" slowly prepares and leads us to the catastrophe, the cruelty of man to man. Lala Kanshi Ram anxiously awaits the Viceroy's announcement. He intuitively feels the dangers that follow the decision to vivisect India. But he consoles himself by recollecting Gandhi's unwillingness "to a division of the country." While the Hindus feel uncertain of their future, the Muslims firmly believe that Pakistan, a separate homeland for them, will definitely be created. Finally, the announcement over the radio comes. Nehru tells the nation that India will be partitioned into two nations and asks the people not to panic and resort to violence and assures "full protection from the government." Then, Lala Kanshi Ram and others "looked at each other and more than regret, more than fear, on the face of each one of them was disbelief."[1] Even before they recover from their disbelief, they hear Jinnah's words: "Pakistan Zindabad! Long live Pakistan." They notice that there was no mercy but only "pride" in the "cry of Jinnah."

Lala Kanshi Ram speaks of the possibility of the Hindus, Sikhs and Muslims living together peacefully as before in Pakistan. But he himself is not convinced of his argument. He adds that they may be allowed to live in Sialkot because the Muslims need them for their economy. While the Hindus, Muslims and Sikhs read their doom in Nehru's announcement, the Muslims see an occasion for celebration. They do it by bursting crackers and taking out processions. Soon, the looting of shops, burning of houses and gruesome murders become order of the day: "Religion ceases to be a humanizing influence. It creates a strong sense of division of separation, so that all who belong to another religion become 'other,' legitimate targets for attack."[2]

Arun realizes that they will be safe only in a refugee camp. Lala Kanshi Ram is shocked when he becomes aware of it. He fondly hopes that he may be able to return to his house and shop one day. He agrees to move to the refugee camp as there alone is "lull" to be found.

The second part presents the storm in all its fury and turbulence. The lull in the lives of Lala Kanshi Ram and the members of his group, however, lasts only for a while. They hear about the horrifying story of the merciless killing of the Hindu and Sikh passengers coming to Sialkot by train. Lala Kanshi Ram is shocked to hear that his daughter Madhu and her husband Rajiv are among those killed. Lala Kanshi Ram's hope of returning to Sialkot is shattered because all the shops belonging to the Hindus have been occupied by the Muslims. He has no choice but to leave for India. He decides to join the foot convoy to Dera Baba Nanak. As Niranjan Singh's beard may invite the wrath of the Muslim fanatics, he is advised to remove it. But instead of making compromise "with his conscience just to survive," he commits self-immolation. During the march, the convoy is ambushed thrice, at Pasrur, Alipur Saiyidian, and Narowal. As a result, many are killed and many refugee girls are abducted. At Narowal, Arun kills Rahmat-Ullah Khan for abducting and raping Sunanda. But he fails to trace Chandni.

Suraj Prakash and Arun see the parade of naked Hindu women. Finally, they set foot on the Indian soil. Lala Kanshi Ram at once sings "Vande Mataram." Arun is also happy: "So they were getting near safety. And freedom. There was something in that. Maybe love would be there too." (271)

But at Amritsar, Lala Kanshi Ram and Arun notice the Hindus being equally communalistic and indulging in similar atrocities as their counterparts in Pakistan. Lala Kanshi Ram hears the wailing of the survivors: "The wailing had a familiar ring, and while many refugees joyfully shouted, 'Serves them right,' Lala Kanshi Ram looked at the ground in humiliation." (275)

From Amritsar, Lala Kanshi Ram, Prabha Rani, Arun, Sunanda and her children go to Delhi with great expectations. But Lala Kanshi Ram is shocked to find the government unable to cope with the influx of millions of refugees. Finally, he reconciles himself to his lot and settles for a brick hutment.

In the third and last part, Gandhi's assassination is reported. A pall of gloom descends over the country. Even the refugees who have lost everything as a result of the havoc caused by the partition consider Gandhi's death "a personal loss." People without any fear of repercussions from the authorities pay homage to Gandhi. But there are some like Bibi Amarvati who say: "And it was Gandhi who sanctioned the partition. . . . Well, it's a good thing he is gone. He brought nothing but misery to us." (306-7)

If '*Azadi*,' freedom, makes people free from alien rule, the partition and the havoc it causes results in "the loss of ability to communicate" in private life. But Nahal, the affirmationist, tells us that suffering, pain, and death are only a prelude to a new life, full of hope. Working at her sewing machine, Sunanda suggests tenacity of the human spirit and a life of action. A study of the novel reveals that taken together, the three parts form a meaningful sequence and there is an underlying unity of structure.

The arrangement of the events and actions, the interaction between the characters involved, the description of incidents and the emphasis on causality reveal Nahal's skill in constructing a well-knit plot. There are no loose threads in the novel. Nahal succeeds in arousing our interest and in creating suspense. The plot is concerned with the vivisection of the country into two sovereign states, India and Pakistan, displacement of millions of people like Lala Kanshi Ram on either side of the dividing border, the journey of Lala Kanshi Ram along with the members of his family and his neighbours from Sialkot to India, their awful and ghastly experiences before they set foot on the Indian soil, their disappointment at their failure to establish their identity by securing an independent house, an address of their own, the reported assassination of Gandhi and the valiant efforts of Lala Kanshi Ram and Sunanda to establish themselves again.

Nahal is at his best in delineating the characters in *Azadi*. N. Radhakrishnan observes: "He shows all the qualities of a mature artist. He does not throw the blame on anybody and doesn't betray anger, remorse and escapism. He presents an earnest study of a people who are caught up in the whirlwind of communal frenzy and for whom every moment means death and doom."[3] As the whole narrative centres round Lala Kanshi Ram, he, in the course of the novel, emerges as larger than life. However, the other characters are also fictionally important and they serve the thematic purpose.

Lala Kanshi Ram is a complacent wholesale grain merchant in Sialkot. He hates the British for what they have done to the country. He calls Bhagat Singh a hero and has regard for Gandhi: "But deeper down, he also admired the British—in any case he enjoyed the safety of the British Raj and hugged it lovingly." (17) Though he thinks that his experiences have given him an edge over others in intelligence, at times he is naive. He believes:

> If the British were going to lose India, it was not because of Gandhi or the awakening amongst the masses; it was because of the tactical error they made in sending out an ugly Viceroy in the crucial days of their Raj. (28)

Lala Kanshi Ram wants freedom but without partition. The facts that the British are in a hurry to grant freedom to India and leave the country and the Rajaji formula forming the basis of negotiations between Gandhi and Jinnah create fear in his mind. He is afraid that the English would rather divide than leave behind a united India. Even if two different nations were created out of a single people, he does not understand why he should leave Sialkot. He believes the Hindus, Sikhs and Muslims can live together in peace as before. But as soon as the news of partition is heard, people

> suddenly become conscious of their religious and ethnic roots, of their being Hindus or Muslims, of their belonging to the majority or minority communities. The feeling of hostility naturally runs high all over the north-western and eastern regions of India. What happened in Sialkot and the neighbouring areas thereafter becomes the tale of every village and town in the affected region.[4]

Lala Kanshi Ram is anguished to hear of the riots. The arrival of the Muslims from the Eastern part of the Punjab and their woe-filled accounts of atrocities committed on them by the Hindus fan the fury of the Muslims. He condemns violence whether it is by the Hindus or by the Muslims. As he becomes alien to the land of his birth, he is forced to seek shelter in a refugee camp. Still, he has faint hope that he will return to the place where his roots lay. But the news of the death of his daughter and her husband at the hands of the communalists leaves him completely shaken: "And yet not once did Lala Kanshi Ram acknowledge defeat. He was benumbed by the event, he fretted, but in the next instant Arun could see him pulling his shoulder up." (177) Thus, it is his fortitude that makes him a noble character. However, when he realizes that the two governments have neither "the power nor the intention of maintaining the minorities in their homes," and are parties to the undeclared civil war, he gives up hope of staying in Sialkot.

Lala Kanshi Ram's long-drawn and arduous march to Dera Baba Nanak begins on 24 September. As the Indian authorities fail to give adequate protection, the convoy is ambushed thrice, many are killed, many women abducted and raped, and at a few places women are paraded naked.

At Amritsar he hears of the mass killings of Muslims and parade of naked Muslim women. While some of the refugees take a vicarious pleasure of vengeance, he is shocked to note how man wherever he is, at times, touches the lowest ebb. And he feels humiliated at this. Lala Kanshi Ram tells his wife that hatred brings nothing back. Forgiveness alone will help restore normality. Echoing Gandhi's words, he declares that he "can't hate the Muslims anymore" though they have committed atrocities on the Hindus in Pakistan. Thus, he implicitly says that the Muslims in India too must forgive the majority community. Here, Nahal makes Kanshi Ram a replica of Gandhi.

But the apathy, corruption and inability of the Indian authorities to provide shelter to the refugees who have lost everything for no fault of theirs makes Lala Kanshi Ram, who is already suffering from "a weariness of the spirit," feel "so naked" and "so defenceless." And it is here that he weeps for the first time in his life. But fortunately, he succeeds in securing a two-room brick-hutment in one of the refugee camps in Delhi. However, his failure to secure a house, an address of his own to establish his identity, weighs heavily upon him. As a result of the man-made calamity, Lala Kanshi Ram not only loses his identity but his ability to communicate with his family. Mohan Jha writes: "Judged from this standpoint, *Azadi* may be interpreted as a plea for the realization and assertion of identity in a world that is cruel enough to push people into the oblivion of anonymity." (42-43) However, he soon regains his cool courage and quiet strength. He realizes that freedom is desirable irrespective of the price as it makes people feel "unrestricted" and "untrammelled." Now, they can hold their heads high.

Arun is another round character created by Nahal. College-going Arun is young, passionate, courageous and affectionate son. Like many young men, Arun is easily attracted by beautiful girls. He mistakes attraction for love and is worried that he is not constant in love. Later, he meets Nur, daughter of Chaudhri Barkat Ali, and is at once attracted by her. As his father and Nur's father happen to be friends, Arun and Nur meet quite often and Nur ultimately returns his love for her. He tells her many a time that if necessary he will embrace Islam for her sake. But noticing the change the partition has brought about, he realizes that it is not the time to think of personal love. He resolves as a dutiful son to accompany his old parents, if they are forced to leave Sialkot. Mohan Jha observes: "in the flush of his youthful romance Arun could have elected to go in for Nur in preference to his parents, but the communal holocaust suddenly makes 'a man' of him, and he chooses to share the joys and sorrows of life with his parents." (40)

Arun is rudely shocked to hear the news of his sister's death. She was "his earliest friend and companion." It is a personal loss to him. But he remembers that life is continuous:

> It was the continuity of life. It was the continuity of the will in the being of things. And never had this urge for survival, for self-assertion, manifested itself in Arun so powerfully as at this time of death. It was as if he would himself perish otherwise. (174)

As Nur is beyond his reach and Madhu is no more, Chandni alone is a certainty. He loves her and boldly tells his mother that he will marry Chandni, the daughter of a charwoman. Later, he manfully kills Captain Rahmat-Ullah Khan for molesting Sunanda. Thus, Arun acquires a new identity for himself. But it is surprising to see him obsessed with Chandni. Her abduction and his failure to trace her makes him listless, sick and demented. Even after he resumes his studies in a college in Delhi, he feels lonely without her. He feels like committing suicide: "But he stayed alive, to feel his hurt. In death he would feel nothing. . . . In that hurt he still had a bond with the girl. Without the hurt the bond might be lost." (305-6)

Arun is aware that it is his duty to console his father who, though upset by Madhu's death, went from pillar to post to secure shelter for them in Delhi. But he fails to communicate with his father, and remains confined to his "own single self."

Among the Muslim characters, Chaudhri Barkat Ali stands out displaying the best in human nature. His is the voice of reason in the novel. His nobility and belief "in the unity of all religions" endear him to one and all. He makes it his job "to live the life God had given him in friendship and love. And the Hindu next door was as much his brother, more his brother, than an unknown Muslim living elsewhere." (86)

After listening to Gandhi's speech, he starts wearing khadi, and becomes a member of the Congress. But he does not force his wife and children to follow suit because he never imposes his will on others. He allows his daughter who is in love with Arun to meet him.

Chaudhri Barkat Ali rightly observes that the arrival of the Muslim refugees from India with stories of heinous crimes committed on them by the Hindus inflames the local Muslims. The local politicians take advantage of it and fan up communal hatred. As a result, the ideal world of mutual friendship and loyalties is shattered. So he advises Lala Kanshi Ram to move to the refugee camp and save themselves from the wrath of the Muslim fanatics. Madhu's death moves him as it does her father. He joins Arun in the latter's efforts to trace the dead bodies of Madhu and her husband. When Ghani speaks disparagingly of the dead, his anger knows no bounds. He catches hold of Ghani's neck and shouts: "You shaitan—you shaitan—you blot on the name of Islam." (156)

On the day of the departure of the foot convoy, Chaudhri Barkat Ali goes with his son to the refugee camp before dawn. They walk with Lala Kanshi Ram's family for six miles. Then Chaudhri Barkat Ali bids farewell to his friend and his family: "There were tears in the eyes of both men. They had nothing more to say, having exhausted themselves of emotion in all these weeks." (232)

While religion is a personal matter for Chaudhri Barkat Ali, it suddenly becomes a factor of segregation for Abdul Ghani. Ghani has been a long time friend of Lala Kanshi Ram and always greets Arun with "Ohai, Arun 'de puter,' how're you?" But the moment, the country is divided on religious lines, the "wiry hookah manufacturer" realizes that it is an opportunity to drive the Hindus out of Pakistan and grab their property. Evidently, he becomes a communalist for economic gains. Asghar Ali Engineer rightly observes: "Religion, or region are not *per se*, the source of violence and hatred; they yield to violence or hatred only when integrally associated with the process of iniquitous development."[5]

Rahmat-Ullah Khan is a sensuous and lascivious Pakistani army officer. He is an old classmate of Arun. But he expresses no sympathy when Arun tells him that his sister became a victim of religious frenzy. He does not condemn the communal killings. However, he promises to help them by including them in the foot convoy. After seeing Sunanda, he becomes enamoured of her. He tells Arun that if he brings her to him, he will take Arun, his father and others in a jeep to Jammu border. Thus, he throws before Arun the bait of "a quick escape from this living inferno." As Arun says no to it, he abducts and rapes her, for which he pays with his death at the hands of Arun.

Sergeant William Davidson, with his courtesy, pleasant tone and love of India reminds us of Sir Kenneth Ashby. He supports the cause of freedom. He knows that the British arguments that "India should prepare herself for freedom" and "the Indians must arrive at their freedom slowly," smack of hypocrisy. He believes that to allow the Indians to "live" "breathe," "exist," and "function" in joy, no preparation is necessary. He says: "And the British used all these arguments only to prolong their stay here—not in the interest of India, but in their own interest." (100) Though Davidson is fascinated by India, he feels it is shameful that the Indians are not unitedly fighting for independence. He honestly tells his Indian friends, Arun and Munir that the division of India is "the most stupid, most damaging, most negative development." He does not mistake Lala Kanshi Ram, when the latter raises his finger against the British for not preventing violence.

Sergeant William Davidson is objective in his estimate of the British rule in India. He says that Wavell mismanaged things and Mountbatten duped them into bifurcation of the country. Having once decided to partition the subcontinent, the British prepare to leave in a hurry. Thus, Davidson admits that the British are self-centred, hypocritical, irresponsible and indifferent. He also finds fault with Gandhi and Jinnah. He says that Gandhi and Jinnah fell "for a handy prize" without realizing the misery the partition would bring to the people. Later, he reveals his helping nature by arranging a truck to take Lala Kanshi Ram and his neighbours to the refugee camp safely. Thus, William Davidson provides the point of view of an enlightened Englishman towards the Indian situation.

Sunanda Bala, the daughter-in-law of Bibi Amarvati, is a ravishing beauty. She is so sensitive that she fears that through touch with others her beautiful body will be defiled. Though her husband Suraj Prakash is "not much good," she loves him. As the future heiress to Bibi Amarvati's property, she always behaves in a dignified manner. She very rarely comes out of her house.

As a result of the partition and the consequential enmity it creates between the Muslims and the others, Lala Kanshi Ram and Bibi Amarvati leave everything behind and move to the refugee camp. While Lala Kanshi Ram feels "defenceless and naked," Sunanda "walked with majesty even in grief, and floated out into the street like a tableau; . . . she walked unconcerned, she walked as though she still owned the world." (129)

While almost everyone, at the refugee camp, is physically and mentally tired under the strain of riots, Sunanda remains her usual self. She is so alert that she understands that Captain Rahmat-Ullah Khan is after her. Without any fear she tells Arun that she will kill Rahmat-Ullah Khan if he ever tries to touch her. However, she breaks into tears when she is abducted and raped by Rahmat-Ullah Khan and when she learns that her husband has been killed in the attack on their camp. She tells Arun: "what is there left of me to lose?" But soon, she regains her composure. She requests Arun not to "say a word" about what he has seen.

Sunanda knows that life is for living and for that one must leave behind past. No amount of brooding over the past will bring back her dead husband. She makes an affirmation by acquiring a used sewing machine and taking up "odd tailoring jobs": "the sewing machine, with all its continuous rhythmic movements, sounds and vibrations also suggests the continuous rhythmic flow of life."[6]

Madhu, daughter of Lala Kanshi Ram and Prabha Rani, is another memorable woman character created by Chaman Nahal.

Though young, she has the courage to face her detractors boldly. As "nothing could easily beat her," she has only contempt for those who tease her about the marks on her face left by smallpox. The moon and stars bewitch her and she becomes ecstatic. She considers the moon "a mysterious beloved" and the stars his lovers. She begins to sing a song and dance to its rhythm. Even after finishing the song she is still "in the throes of its impact." Madhu is so intelligent that there are "infinite facets to her wit." She holds Arun, her younger brother, in arms and talks to him of all kinds of subjects. Her affection makes Arun consider her a "friend and companion." But the young and vivacious Madhu and her husband Rajiv, along with hundreds of others, are killed by communalists while they are coming from Wazirabad to Sialkot. Man's wolfish cruelty to man in the name of religion takes a heavy toll of innocent people like Madhu.

Though Gandhi does not appear in person in *Azadi*, his visit to Sialkot is vividly recalled by Chaudhri Barkat Ali. His recapitulation of Gandhi's visit and the latter's speech throws light on Gandhi's personality and impact on people. Gandhi comes to Sialkot in 1930, in the course of his tour of the Punjab. Chaudhri Barkat Ali attends the meeting with his friend Lala Kanshi Ram.

Gandhi's Champaran agitation revolutionizes "the spirit of the country" and he becomes a household name in every city. He talks of peace and non-violence. He explains to them the meaning of 'purna swaraj,' India's "long history of self-discipline to fight for full '*Azadi*' non-violently." The British have two sets of laws, one for them and another for their colonies. They speak of freedom at home and deny the same to the colonized. In spite of it, Gandhi hates the British rule and not the British. He further says that the Hindu-Muslim unity and non-violence must form the basis for self-discipline and self-sacrifice. He further says:

> let each Muslim accept one Hindu as his 'brother,' and the Hindu that Muslim as his brother. And from today . . . wear home-made things and not those imported from England. (89)

Gandhi's speech inspires Chaudhri Barkat Ali and his ilk. He at once turns towards Lala Kanshi Ram and declares that he is his brother from that day. He decides to wear khadi and become a member of the Congress.

Unlike in the earlier volumes of *The Gandhi Quartet*, Nahal in *Azadi* employs multiple or shifting points of view as it

> helps the reader realize the full meaning of the great historical event, namely the Partition of an-age-old sub-continent into two countries, India and Pakistan. Presented through two centres of consciousness, a great political event is transformed into a powerful human drama enacted not only on a geo-physical or socio-economic stage but also in the theatres of the home and the hearth, in the theatres of the mind and the soul.[7]

Though all the characters in the novel experience similar traumatic effects of the partition, it is the varying reactions of Lala Kanshi Ram and Arun that become centre of interest. Lala Kanshi Ram's ambiguous attitude to the British 'Raj,' his failure to foresee the true dimensions of Hindu-Muslim hostilities, his shock when he learns that he has become a refugee in his own city, the extremely painful experiences at the refugee camp and the news of his daughter's death benumb him. Still, he is not defeated: "His individual consciousness has in the end matured and developed into a national consciousness, rather a purely humanistic consciousness."[8]

Arun's point of view helps to dramatize more intensely the throes of partition. Further, it helps the novelist to introduce William Davidson and through him present the British attitude to partition. But M.K. Naik points out: "Another serious flaw is the mixing up of the point of view of the protagonist, Lala Kanshi Ram and that of Arun, which destroys the unity of impression."[9]

While describing the events, Nahal's viewpoint is always on the essential nature of man. So he presents both man's weaknesses and strengths. At Narowal, the Muslims parade naked Hindu women. As the procession moved, "a river of obscenities—foul abuses, crude personal gestures, spurts of sputum, odd articles like small coins, faded flowers, cigarette butts and bidis that were thrown at the women." (250) Man seems to be same everywhere. At Amritsar the Hindus take out a procession of Muslim women through the bazaar.

But there are a few who with their kindness add meaning to life. At Narowal, the Hakim weeps for the women who are being paraded naked. Lala Kanshi Ram and other refugees are scared while they near Jassar, a Muslim village:

> But so pitiable was the sight of this demoralized mass of humanity, which moved on its way accompanied by a swarm of flies, the Muslims in Jassar only stood and stared. Even anti-Hindu or anti-Sikh slogans were not shouted by them. The men stood astounded, as group after group of disabled, wounded, or weeping and lamenting men and women turned the bend, came before them. . . . Instead of attacking the convoy, some of the inhabitants of Jassar ran inside the homes and brought water for the thirsty. Some waved and said, 'Khuda hafiz.' Most only looked on. (269)

Thus, Nahal records both the hatred and spontaneous overflow of compassion of the people.

Nahal gives a realistic account of both the political and social India. The historical events referred to in the novel are the Viceroy Lord Mountbatten's announcement over the radio on 3 June 1947 with regard to the freedom and much talked about partition, Nehru's speech that confirms the worst fears of the minorities everywhere, victory march by the Muslims, the age-old communal harmony giving place to hatred and destruction of human attributes, establishment of refugee camps, the announcement of Boundary Commission's Award which allows the refugees realize where they are—"on a part of Pakistan, or of India," the mass exodus, rehabilitation of millions of uprooted families and Gandhi's assassination on 30 January 1948. The novel roughly covers a period of eight months and things move at monstrous speed.

Nahal's *Azadi* also abounds in social realism without which the novel would remain a mere record of historical events. Amidst murder, arson, loot and rape perpetrated by man, there always stand people like Lala Kanshi Ram and the Hakim who forgive and preach tolerance. Human kindness even in the midst of bloodbath is the theme of the novel. It is the only hope for man's survival. Nahal gives an account of the Dussehra festival held every year at Sialkot. Almost all Indians are inquisitive and they cannot curb the tendency of making enquiries even about strangers. Arun asks Bill Davidson about the latter's marriage, brothers and sisters. Nahal shows how selfish man is when Abdul Ghani repeatedly asks Lala Kanshi Ram, his long time friend, when he will be leaving Sialkot so that he can occupy his shop. Religion not only divides people but makes some barbarians. While Arun is trying to locate the dead bodies of his sister and her husband, Abdul Ghani says:

> Who told you your sister was killed, my boy? But don't worry, I put her and her husband into the fire with my own hands, and they're now on their way to dozakh, to hell—where I hope they rot for ever! (155)

After their horrifying experiences during their march to India, the refugees expect every kind of help from the Indian authorities in getting them rehabilitated. But their apathy and corruption shock Lala Kanshi Ram.

Nahal's characteristic use of language in the novel also lends a touch of realism to his historical narrative. He freely uses native Hindi words and also Punjabi swear words adding thereby, a touch of nativity. To cite but a few lines:

> "Oh, they're kutai, they're dogs—these angrez." (19)
> "Lalaji, thik hai?" (23)
> "Han sahib, thik hun. Bilkul thik hun, sahib." (23)
> "Nothing much, chachiji. I'm only making bhurta." (38)
> "Eh, behen chode!" said Lala Kanshi Ram slowly. . . (19)
> "I hope they don't—these badmash!" (40)

While giving exquisite pictures of Sunanda and Madhu Bala, both drawn in recapitulation, Nahal's language turns lyrical. His beautiful pen-picture of Sunanda concludes with the words: "She was not a human being, she was a presence." Nahal gives a memorable portrait of the playful girl, Madhu. She sings a song of K.L. Sehgal and under its impact goes into a trance.

Another instance of Nahal's remarkable use of language is his successful presentation of the deep psychic disturbances brought about by the traumatic experience. Nur sees no hope of meeting Arun again and it hurts her. She writes a letter and sends it through her brother: "The letter was not only smudgy with her tears; the whole paper seemed to have been dipped in the sadness of her heart." (224) The lines reveal pathos, bitter agony, and misfortune and it is such lines that elevate prose to verse.

Nahal makes a good use of the technique of contrast in order to make the narrative effective. The contrast is at two levels—characters and events. Niranjan Singh and Gangu Mull are a contrast to each other. While the former is prepared to lose his head rather than his faith, the latter converts himself to Islam to save his property. Another instance of notable contrast is between Abdul Ghani, a religious bigot and an opportunist, and Chaudhri Barkat Ali, the apostle of religious harmony. Chaudhri Barkat Ali is sad to see Lala Kanshi Ram and his family leaving Sialkot and offers words of consolation. On the other hand, Abdul Ghani, though a friend of Lala Kanshi Ram, anxiously awaits the latter's departure so that he can usurp his property. There are contrasts between events also. The cordial relationship that existed between the Hindus and the Muslims in the pre-partition days is contrasted with the animosity between the Hindus and Muslims of post-partition days.

In addition to contrasts, there are parallels in the novel. Both the Muslim and the Hindu refugees experience hell before they reach their destination. The Muslim refugees from India and the Indian refugees from Pakistan do not feel happy even after reaching their separate homelands. The protection provided to the convoys of refugees on either side is only half-hearted.

Chaman Nahal's use of imagery and symbolism in *Azadi*

compels our attention. The three parts of the novel "The Lull," "The Storm," and "The Aftermath" indicate the image of sea in its three stages, namely calm before storm, storm, and calm after storm. K.C. Belliappa rightly observes: "Nahal perceptively shows how suffering, pain and death is only a prelude to a new life, full of affirmation and hope. This is symbolically brought out in the birth of a child to Isher Kaur on the train."[10]

Till they reach Delhi, Lala Kanshi Ram and other refugees firmly believe that it will be their sanctuary. But as Lala Kanshi Ram's hopes are belied, he does not consider Delhi a land of peace and hope. It hurts him so much that he stops wearing turban, the symbol of dignity. As Lala Kanshi Ram passes through Kurukshetra, the battle-field of the Pandavas and the Kauravas of the epic *Mahabharata*, he feels that the Hindus, the Sikhs and the Muslims are waging a similar battle because of hatred, animosity and revenge. After so much destruction on either side, no one is the real winner. As Lala Kanshi Ram is convinced of the futility of hatred, he resolves not to hate anyone.

Nahal's use of irony makes *Azadi* an intensely dramatic novel. There is a central irony operating on the concept of '*Azadi*' or freedom at political, social and personal levels. At the political level, the attainment of '*Azadi*' only brings misery to everyone. It wipes out the dream of living in harmony as one free nation. It seems to be a mockery of freedom as it results in the division of the country, mass killings and exodus. It makes a travesty of "heaven of freedom" that is described by Tagore in his poem which forms the epigraph of *Azadi*.

At the social level the religious divide makes beasts of men and they behave in the most undignified manner. There is no dignity even in death: "The dead had been removed from the train and dumped without sentiment or concern." (155) Those who escape abduction and molestation are separated from their kith and kin. Thus '*Azadi*' results in the loss of their property, social position, the beloveds and their very identity. Religiously, '*Azadi*' results in rancour between the Hindus and the Muslims.

At the personal level, '*Azadi*' shatters the hopes, dreams and aspirations of almost all. Lala Kanshi Ram, an established grain merchant, becomes a refugee in his own place, loses his daughter and is forced to become a witness to the worst in human nature. Arun fails to realize his dream of happy marriage to Nur at first and with Chandni later. Chaudhri Barkat Ali's dream of Hindu-Muslim unity and Niranjan Singh's dream of perpetual allegiance to 'Guru Maharaj' are made impossible as a result of the hostilities created by the partition. Above all, the suffering brought by '*Azadi*' and the partition makes Lala Kanshi Ram, Prabha Rani and Arun desolate and they find it impossible to open their hearts to one another as "the contact was broken."

Though a thoroughgoing realist, Nahal is essentially an affirmationist. He is of the firm view, that life is worth living with all its vicissitudes. He does not fail to project his affirmation of life even in a grave novel like *Azadi* dealing as it does with the holocaust of partition.

Though partition seems to have wiped out the dream of living a free and happy life in post-Independence India, Nahal is able to see a silver line in the cloudy sky. For Nahal, partition is the beginning of transformation for people like Lala Kanshi Ram and his son Arun. After seeing the evil and violence on both sides, Lala Kanshi Ram says: "We are all equally guilty." As many refugees kiss the Indian soil after crossing the bridge over Ravi and bathe in the river to mark their deliverance, Lala Kanshi Ram raises his hand and shouts "Vande Mataram—salute to the Motherland." Despite their failure to get a house, Arun and his father feel contented with the accommodation they acquire at the refugee camp. Arun is happy that at least they are free now. Lala Kanshi Ram is impressed by the pride with which each man stands in the post-Independence India. He is happy that people are now "firm, evenly balanced and sure of themselves." Without any fear of persecution, they mourn the death of Gandhi. Nahal's philosophy of life is that suffering, pain and death are only a prelude to a new life, full of hope and affirmation.

II

A study of Nahal's *Azadi* compels one's attention to Manohar Malgonkar's *A Bend in the Ganges* (1964), Khushwant

Singh's *Train to Pakistan* (1956), and Bhisham Sahni's *Tamas* (1974) which also deal with the theme of partition. These novels, like *Azadi*, reveal how people, affected by communal virus, behave like beasts. They depict how people suddenly forget the camaraderie and bonhomie that have existed among them till yesterday and start killing one another in the name of religion. They also describe how millions of people become refugees overnight in the land of their birth. For instance, Malgonkar in *A Bend in the Ganges* tells us how

> A week ago they had all been citizens of India; men and women jubilant at the advent of the long-awaited, long fought for freedom. Today, they were just a small section of a seething movement of humanity. Here they were the Muslims, the counterparts of the 'displaced persons' on the other side, who were Hindus and Sikhs. . . . They were, at the moment stateless citizens, hounded out from the land of their birth as much by collective fear of racial massacres as by the actual outrages perpetrated upon them by their erstwhile fellow-citizens. Political expediency had suddenly transformed them into refugees. . . . They left behind everything they possessed; their lands, houses. . . . They also left behind scores of thousands of dead and dying, sacrificial offerings to freedom.[11]

Again, like Nahal, Malgonkar, Khushwant Singh and Bhisham Sahni subscribe to the view that life is worth living with all its vicissitudes—hatred, lootings, abductions, rapes and killings. To cite but a few instances, in *A Bend in the Ganges*, Gian Talwar and Sundari notice that the latter's father, Tekchand, is missing. They understand that he has gone back to their home to perform the last rites of his wife who has been murdered by Shafi, a communalist. Gian Talwar and Sundari realize that they cannot hold up the convoy of refugees for the sake of Tekchand: "For a second or two Gian hesitated. Then he started the engine and threw the car into gear while Mulligan kept motioning him forward with his arm. Then, without looking at Sundari, he released the clutch. The Ford leaped forward." (382)

In *Train to Pakistan*, Juggat Singh learns of the plan of the Sikhs to attack the train going to Pakistan near the bridge in Mano Majra. The train, along with hundreds of Muslim refugees, is also carrying the pregnant Nooran, Juggat's beloved. He resolves that though Nooran cannot live with him in Mano Majra, she must at least live separately in the newly created Pakistan. So he heroically cuts the rope tied across the bridge and allows the train to go over to Pakistan: "The train went over him, and went on to Pakistan."[12]

In *Tamas*, when the Muslim rioters ask Iqbal Singh whether he chooses death or conversion to Islam, the latter agrees to embrace Islam:

> Before nightfall all the signs of Iqbal Singh's Sikhism had been carefully obliterated, in their place were all the external Muslim signs. From an enemy he had been transformed into a friend, not an infidel, but a believer—a 'Mussalman.' The doors of all Muslim houses were now open to him.[13]

Similarly, Prakasho, who has been kidnapped by Alla Rakha, refuses to eat anything offered by him because he is a Muslim. However, on the fourth day she realizes that either she should live with him or face death. As she decides to live with him, she accepts the 'burfi' given by him: "Timidly Prakasho hugged him back. She was amazed to find herself actually enjoying herself." (224)

Also, like Chaman Nahal, Malgonkar, Khushwant Singh and Bhisham Sahni do not hold any single individual responsible for the tragedies that unfold in the wake of splitting the subcontinent into two independent nations.

All the same, a discerning reader notices that *Azadi*, more than any other novel on the theme of India's partition, stresses the profound significance of human life and provides an integral view of life. What, according to K. Venkata Reddy, the novel seeks to present is how man is the victim of forces of history. Nonetheless, "there is a note of hope and affirmation of life. Underlying the awful irony of the stupendous drama of history is the author's positive attitude manifested in the showing of futility of hatred and triumph of love."[14]

After the holocaust of partition, Lala Kanshi Ram and other refugees from Pakistan realize that they can live more honourably as human beings in independent India. As soon as they hear the news of Gandhi's assassination,

> They wept too loudly or they shouted loudly. Today the men stood in pride—evenly balanced, firm, sure of themselves. Unlike the past, there was no leader urging them to demonstrate their feelings. The feelings had their own recourse. Lala Kanshi Ram raised his head with pride and stretched back his shoulders. He was unrestricted now, he was untrammelled. (309)

To cite another example, in the wake of partition, Sunanda loses her husband and is abducted and raped by Captain Rahmat-Ullah Khan at Narowal. However, "her honour remained intact, though in her mind . . . and so innocent and dove like did she look, as though through some miraculous process she had not only been restored to her wholeness but also to her virginity." (307) On hearing the news of Gandhi's death, she says: "It does hurt, mother. Men like him come once in centuries." (307)

Thus, *Azadi*, like other novels dealing with the holocaust of India's partition, occupies a special place in Indian English fiction.

At a time, when extreme inhumanity often finds its justification in religion and when we seem to be returning to the world of the Partition, with its massacre of innocent people, it would be worth the while to read these novels depicting the "sweeping, shattering saga of the colossal tragedy and disruption that accompanied the partition and independence in the Indian subcontinent."[15] They help us to recollect the past and may induce us not to repeat it. As Salman Rushdie rightly observes: "Those who forget the past are condemned to repeat it."[16]

NOTES

1. Chaman Nahal, *Azadi* (1979; New Delhi: Orient Paperbacks, 1988), vol. 4 of *The Gandhi Quartet* (New Delhi: Allied, 1993), p. 56.
2. Shirin L. Kudchedkar, "The Second Coming: Novels of the Partition," *Indian English Fiction: 1980-90: An Assessment* (Delhi: B.R., 1994), pp. 63-64.
3. N. Radhakrishnan, *Indo-Anglian Fiction: Major Trends and Themes* (Madras: Emerald , 1984), p. 65.
4. Mohan Jha, "Chaman Nahal's *Azadi*: A Search for Identity," *Studies in Indian Fiction in English*, ed. G.S. Balarama Gupta (Gulbarga: JIWE, 1987), pp. 36-37.
5. Asghar Ali Engineer, *Communalism and Communal Violence in India* (Delhi: Ajanta, 1989), p. 68.
6. K.K. Sharma and B.K. Johri, "The Epic and Psychological Delineation of the Theme," *The Partition in Indian English Novels* (Ghaziabad: Vimal, 1984), p. 116.
7. K.S. Ramamurti, "*Azadi*—Point of View as Technique," *Three Contemporary Novelists*, ed. R.K. Dhawan (New Delhi: Classical, 1985), pp. 131-32.
8. *Ibid*., p. 133.
9. M.K. Naik, *A History of Indian English Literature* (New Delhi: Sahitya Akademi, 1982), p. 232.
10. K.C. Belliappa, "The Elusive Classic: Khushwant Singh's *Train to Pakistan* and Chaman Nahal's *Azadi*," *The Literary Criterion*, 15.2 (1980), p. 70.
11. Manohar Malgonkar, *A Bend in the Ganges* (New Delhi: Orient Paperbacks, 1964), pp. 354-55.
12. Khushwant Singh, *Train to Pakistan* (New Delhi: Ravi Dayal, 1988), p. 207.
13. Bhisham Sahni, *Tamas*, trans. Jai Ratan (1981; New Delhi: Penguin India, 1988), p. 192.
14. K. Venkata Reddy, "The Novelist as Affirmationist: The Achievement of Chaman Nahal," *Critical Studies in Commonwealth Literature* (New Delhi: Prestige, 1994), pp. 165-66.
15. Mulk Raj Anand, Back cover page, *Azadi*.
16. Qtd. R.S. Pathak, "History of the Individual in the Novels of Rushdie," *Three Contemporary Novelists*, ed. R.K. Dhawan (New Delhi: Classical, 1985), p. 216.

Have Faith: The "Epilogue"

When Nahal wrote *Azadi* which deals with the partition of India and the awful and ghastly experience of millions of refugees and *The Crown and the Loincloth* which narrates the first mass movement, he did not have the intention of writing *The Gandhi Quartet.* Even in 1985, he said that he would be writing two more novels narrating the second and third phases of India's struggle for freedom and complete the trilogy. But after writing *The Salt of Life* which concerns itself with the historic Dandi March, he said that he was working "on *The Triumph of the Tricolour*, the last of his novels based on India's freedom movement. Together, when completed, the four novels will be issued as *The Gandhi Quartet.*"[1] Accordingly, after writing *The Triumph of the Tricolour,* he reworked the four novels into *The Gandhi Quartet.* Consequently, *Azadi* which was written earlier than the other three novels, became the last volume of *The Gandhi Quartet.* However, Nahal added an "Epilogue" to the 1993 edition of *Azadi* with the main purpose of connecting the four novels.

The "Epilogue" gives a brief description of the post-Independence political India. It throws ample light on Kusum, Vikram, Amit, Ginger Cutlass, Carol Schnicke, Dr. Fogelson and Matthew Craig—the characters who appeared in the first three volumes of *The Gandhi Quartet.*

Nahal begins the "Epilogue" by giving a brief account of the events that took place between 1948 and 1952. India becomes a republic having only nominal links with England. Many princely states including Lambini are merged with India, and a few with Pakistan. Along with other princely states, Lambini has changed much.

Amit is now nearing twenty and working as a teacher in the Lambini Public School, Angela Davis is its Principal and her husband, Kenneth Ashby, its Manager. Vikram is now thirty-five and lives permanently at Sevagram. After Gandhi's assassination, he takes it upon his shoulders to continue many of "the Mahatma's activities." Julie is elected as a Member of Parliament from Ajmer, and is "an important functionary in the Nehru Government." Padamrai Kranti, the tribal leader, is now an M.P. The fifty-four-year-old Kusum lives in her palace at Lambini. She is busy looking after her personal property and the school.

Lala Kanshi Ram and Prabha Rani are living in Delhi. After finishing college, Arun becomes a journalist. Lala Kanshi Ram always forces memories of Madhu on his wife, which the latter would like to obliterate.

Amit makes his own choice and decides to marry Shalini, a tribal girl. After Sunil and Vikram, it is now Amit who disappoints and hurts Kusum. As she starts crying, she hears Bapu's voice telling her: "Have faith." The words soothe her and a smile spreads on her face.

Brigadier Alan Cutlass and his wife, Ginger Cutlass, live in London. But David, Ginger's divorced husband, is still serving the Indians. Ginger is not quite pleased with her daughter Lucy's decision to join David in India. Julie's parents, Dr. Fogelson and Judith Fogelson, are at Cambridge. The former sets up "a small practice for himself," just outside the town. He intends to collect the photographs which he believes will represent the unity and cordiality that existed between the British and the Indians. Matthew Craig, soon after the war ends, returns to Louisville. He is now interested in gambling and not in Gandhi. Carol Schnicke, despite heavy losses in her Brisbane mines, runs her crisis centre for destitutes at Fremantle in Australia. Their stay at Fremantle does a lot of good to Jennifer and Percy Wand. Carol Schnicke and John Tree become lovers. However, they do not marry, but live in concord.

Nahal arranges the incidents in the "Epilogue" in such a way that it acquires an analyzable form and meaning. If *The Gandhi Quartet* is the story of freedom movement led by Gandhi, it is the story of Kusum, the fictional heroine, as well.

Nahal devotes almost the entire "Epilogue" to Kusum. It tells us how Kusum is once again a disappointed woman because Vikram decides to stay in Sevagram and continue the work that is dear to the late lamented Gandhi.. Amit goes against the wishes of his mother and marries a tribal girl. As a result, Kusum begins to feel hurt and lonely. She even contemplates suicide. At this juncture, Bapu's voice tells her to "have faith." The words help her regain her composure.

Nahal's portrayal of Kusum reveals that he prefers "showing" to "telling" as a method of revealing character because "this method unlocks the life in characters rather than treating them as inanimate objects. Moreover we feel that *we* decide what a character is like when we observe him or her behaving in front of us, we can use our critical intelligence and our knowledge of human beings to reach an assessment of them. Whereas when we are told something we can only take it or leave it."[2]

Kusum is "imperial and regal" even at fifty-five. She lives at Lambini. She is busy looking after the Lambini Public School, a co-educational institution started on Bapu's advice. After the death of her second husband, Raja Vishal Chand, she pinned her hopes on her sons. Like most mothers, Kusum expected her sons to stay with her and marry the girls of her choice. But she was disappointed because Vikram married Julie, an English woman. Now, she is once again a disappointed mother because Amit, much against her wishes, chooses Shalini, a tribal girl, as his bride. Kusum tries to get some solace by seeing the bride "decked in jewellery" in their Punjabi tradition. But she feels frustrated when Shalini tells her that Santhals wear no ornaments except beads and glass bangles.

The totally strange marriage rituals of the tribals make Kusum fear Amit's safety. She is afraid that Shalini is a witch and Amit is going to enter an unknown region. She feels helpless and begins to pity herself: "I have been so badly whipped by the two husbands I married, by the two sons I produced, if Amit is profligate, is Vikram any better?"[3] She bursts into tears and behaves like an ordinary woman. Thus, it is evident that though Kusum is the leading fictional character in *The Gandhi*

Quartet, Nahal has no intention of idealizing her. She says:

> I used to be so firm once, had such firm views, they called me cold and unfeeling for that firmness, but now I seem to falter, may be it's my age, may be it's my fears. (363)

But soon, the maternal affection for her children makes Kusum forgive their son's perfunctory attitude to her. She prays to God: "please have mercy on my boys, . . . please have mercy on us one and all, please have mercy on Shalini, please let Amit and Shalini be happy!" (363) At this stage, she hears someone telling her: "Have faith." She, at once, realizes that it is Bapu's voice:

> Yes it was the same voice, with the same tenor, the same modulation, the same pitch; it had the same urgency in it, the same conviction, the same little slur of the tongue. (364)

The words soothe her agitated mind and she is no longer gloomy.

In Vikram, Nahal presents one who is really interested in continuing the work that is dear to Gandhi. Vikram, after the assassination of Gandhi, starts living at Sevagram. As Julie does not join him, he remains alone. Added to it, there are very few who are willing to join him in spreading Gandhian ideals. However, these developments do not deter him from visiting places and preaching love, tolerance and harmony.

As long as the British imperialists stayed in India, they bled the country, set one Indian against another to safeguard imperial interests and divided the country into two independent nations before they were edged out of India. But all the while, they claimed that their aim was not exploitation but protection of the interests of Indians. Even after quitting India, they say the same. Nahal illustrates how hypocritical they are by giving the example of Dr. Fogelson. The latter decides to collect the old regimental and civilian photographs and display them to the world so that "They give a complete lie to the talk of our [the British] exploiting the natives." (326)

India continues to be a money spinner to Alan and Ginger, who make a living through selling paintings depicting India. In spite of it they say: "that cesspool of heat and filth! . . . Its people have no values, . . . they are just a crowd!" (324)

Lest we should conclude that all Englishmen are selfish, ungrateful and hypocritical, Nahal introduces Lucy and David who remain grateful to India where they lived for many years. Lucy differs with Ginger, her mother's views about India and resolves to join her father, David, who is still serving India.

Nahal gives a sad but a true picture of post-Independence India. Even by 1952 that is just four years after the death of Gandhi, many Congressmen lost their commitment to the ideology of Gandhi. It is shocking to see that those Congress leaders who have come to power in the name of Mahatma have "unashamedly put self before service and even flaunted the extent of their jail terms or the number of lathi blows they might have received for the rewards they wanted." (349) And "service in itself was a forgotten memory for them." (349) However, fortunately, there are at least a handful of people who have the welfare of India at heart and the desire to serve the nation. Some of those few are Kusum, Vikram, Lucy and David. It is they who keep the nation moving in spite of poverty and want prevailing almost everywhere.

As part of his narrative technique, Nahal employs third person point of view in the "Epilogue." It is "narrated by an author who knows everything about his characters and who is able to follow processes of thought normally hidden from everyone except the thinker."[4]

Nahal makes an effective use of the internal monologue to describe Kusum's mixed reactions to Amit's wedding. Nahal shows Kusum talking to herself about her disappointment, fears over Amit's future as the husband of a tribal girl, her reconcilement with Amit's choice and finally her desire that Vikram and Amit should lead happy lives.

Though *The Gandhi Quartet* is historical, Nahal brings in the element of fantasy. Kusum who is feeling lonely, hurt and unhappy hears the voice of Gandhi, who had died four years earlier, telling her: "Have faith." The words thrill her and all her unhappiness vanishes. Nahal introduces this fantasy to thrill the readers and tell Kusum and, thereby, everyone of the need to repose faith in Gandhian ideology. This particular narrative device "demands an additional adjustment because of the oddness of its method or subject matter."[5]

Nahal's implied suggestion, that a return to Gandhi is what Kusum needs, introduces into *The Gandhi Quartet* the element of prophecy which, as E.M. Forster notes, is "a tone of voice," demanding as it does "humility and the suspension of the sense of humour."

That Nahal revels in writing long sentences, is once again evidenced in the "Epilogue." While describing Kusum's feeling of hurt, fears over Amit's safety, reconciliation with his choice of the tribal girl as his bride and prayer to God to have mercy on all of them, Nahal writes a sentence containing three hundred and ten lines (355-63).

Nahal lends a touch of nativity to the narration by making Prabha Rani frequently recite rural Punjabi proverbs such as "An old mare should seek no red ruins!" "If I'm a queen, and you are a queen too, who will fetch water?" "Mother and father are weeds, but the son is blossom!" Songs constitute an important part of marriage festivities in India and more so in Punjab. Nahal makes Kusum and her companions sing a Punjabi marriage song:

> There goes the ride
> To the bridegroom's side
> To his bed she goes
> To his heart
> Where else would she now bide! (346)

The novelist gives a graphic account of the Indian political scene in the 1950s. Soon after Gandhi's death, many of his followers become seekers of power and are interested only in feathering their own nests. Very few visit Sevagram. Nahal also gives a vivid picture of the rituals the Santhals, one of the many tribes in India, perform during the marriage of Shalini and

Amit. As J.K. Galbraith rightly observes: "Nahal is full of the flavour of India, the Punjab and the time."[6]

In Nahal's *The Gandhi Quartet*, Gandhi's voice urging Kusum to "have faith" creates uncertainty among the readers. When we take into consideration Kusum's long association with Gandhi, how she sought refuge, when in distress, in the presence of Gandhi and her faith in Gandhian ideology, it is not unreasonable to conclude that she feels it to be the voice of Gandhi comforting and encouraging her. Faith might be interpreted as faith in her children, in herself, in Gandhi's precepts and perhaps in the ultimate higher destiny of man. It may even be that Nahal wishes to conclude his *The Gandhi Quartet* with an implied message that Gandhi is relevant today.

In the 30s and the 40s, Gandhi fought not only for freedom of the country, but worked for Hindu-Muslim unity, removal of untouchability, prohibition of liquor, regeneration of villages and emancipation of women. He lived with the poor before he claimed to be for them. He brought on to the centrestage of political and public life truth, non-violence and morality. Though intensely religious, he remained secular and never used religion for political ends.

Today, India faces many problems. Independence born out of two-nation theory and partition has intensified religious animosity. The tide of communalism is on the rise. Though given the benefits of reservation, the lot of the poor has not improved, economically or socially. Even the ordinary citizen has established himself more deeply in unscrupulous selfishness and the worship of Mammon is assuming alarming proportions. Probity in public life has taken a back seat and criminalization of politics is the order of the day. In this context, only a Mahatma can redeem the nation back on the path of rectitude, self-sacrifice and simplicity. In other words, Gandhi and his teachings are even more relevant today than they were in the days when political and moral stalwarts like Nehru and Patel were at the helm of affairs. Mulk Raj Anand rightly observes: "Gandhi had given his life to alleviation of the human condition. That concern is still necessary for us to feel, and the work of amelioration has to be our national policy."[7]

II

The triumph of faith is the keynote of the "Epilogue" to *Azadi* like that of Bernard Shaw's *Saint Joan* (1924), T.S. Eliot's *Murder in the Cathedral* (1935) and R.K. Narayan's *The Guide* (1958).

In *Saint Joan*, Joan has tremendous faith in the voices she hears and God. She has an equally great faith in her own destiny as the deliverer of France from the English occupation. She has faith that she would ultimately crown the Dauphin in the Cathedral of Rheims. Even when she is about to be burnt, she does not give up her faith. In the "Epilogue" she says: "My sword shall conquer yet: the sword that never struck a blow."[8]

In T.S. Eliot's *Murder in the Cathedral* also, the theme of faith finds its fullest expression. Becket spurns the temptations of love of pleasure, love of worldly authority, the pursuit of revenge and pursuit of martyrdom so that he might be "the lowest on earth, to be high in heaven." As Tony Bareham observes: "Out of the rejection of these temptations comes the strongest and best faith. When he realizes that Christian martyrdom cannot be the effect of a man's will Becket is truly ready to accept his destiny, for now his faith is complete."[9] As Becket says:

> To the Law of God above the Law of Man.
> Unbar the door! unbar the door!
> We are not here to triumph by fighting,
> by stratagem, or by resistance,
> Not to fight with beasts as men. We have fought the beast
> And have conquered. We have only to conquer
> Now, by suffering. This is the easier victory.
> Now is the triumph of the Cross[10]

Raju, the protagonist of R.K. Narayan's *The Guide* is a cheat who never does anything for others. But towards the end, he is moved by the thought of gratitude of the people who touch his feet. He decides not to cheat them, but fast and pray for rains "thoroughly." Soon he develops faith that his self-sacrifice may bring much-needed rain. On the fourteenth day of his prayer, he "looked about and said, 'Velan, it's raining in the hills. I can feel it coming up under my feet, up my legs—' He sagged down."[11] As C.D. Narasimhaiah observes: "the ending is smooth and inevitable. India's undying faith in God and goodness, holymen and miracles is here rendered quite credible by the novelist's art even to the sceptical and questioning mind."[12]

In Chaman Nahal's *The Gandhi Quartet,* the words "have faith" spoken by Gandhi's voice make "a wonder, a smile spread on Kusum's face." Evidently, her deep sense of disappointment has given place to regeneration of faith in herself, her children and in Gandhian ideology. As she has found her faith once again, we may conclude that she would once again become Kusum, the 'Shakti.'

The coronation of the Dauphin and driving out of the English from the French soil signifies the ultimate triumph of Joan's faith in the voices and God. Becket's eventual realization that he can conquer only by suffering indicates his triumph because his faith in God is now complete and soon there will be one more martyr. The fact that Raju begins to fast and pray in earnest for rains denotes the triumph of the innocent and implicit faith the rain-starved villagers reposed in him. When, on the fourteenth day of his fast, Raju notices that it is raining in the distant hills, it symbolizes the triumph of his faith in himself. When Kusum recovers faith in Gandhi, she regains her composure and begins to smile. It signifies her revival of faith in Gandhi and the tremendous impact it has on her.

NOTES

1. Back flap, Chaman Nahal, *The Salt of Life* (New Delhi: Allied, 1990).
2. Jeremy Hawthorn, *Studying the Novel: An Introduction* (New Delhi: Universal Book Stall, 1992), pp. 49-50.
3. Chaman Nahal, "Epilogue," *Azadi*, vol. 4 of *The Gandhi Quartet* (New Delhi: Allied, 1993), p. 358.
4. Ian Milligan, *The Novel in English: An Introduction* (1983; London: Macmillan, 1987), p. 58.

5. E.M. Forster, *Aspects of the Novel* (1927; London: Edward Arnold, 1953), p. 102.
6. John Kenneth Galbraith, Back flap, "Epilogue" to *Azadi*.
7. Mulk Raj Anand, "Is Gandhi relevant today?" *Newsletter*, Oct. 91-March 92, p. 11.
8. Bernard Shaw, *Saint Joan*, ed. A.C. Ward (1954; Madras: Orient Longman, 1976), p. 183.
9. Tony Bareham, *T.S. Eliot: Murder in the Cathedral* (Essex: Longman York Press, 1981), p. 43.
10. T.S. Eliot, *Murder in the Cathedral,* ed. Nevill Coghill (London: Faber and Faber, 1965), pp. 79-80.
11. R.K. Narayan, *The Guide* (1958; Mysore: Indian Thought Publications, 1988), p. 247.
12. "R.K. Narayan's *The Guide*," *Aspects of Indian Writing in English*, ed. M.K. Naik (Madras: Macmillan, 1979), p. 192.

Conclusion

Gandhian ideology has its roots in the eternal human values, handed down to us over centuries, such as love, truth, non-violence, righteousness, and tolerance. His ideology accommodates many contemporary issues like untouchability, religious harmony, rural poverty and the status of women in society. Srinivasa Iyengar writes:

> To Gandhi, national realization included the ending of political subjection and economic degradation, the removal of social inequalities and abuses like untouchability, caste arrogance, occupational prejudices, etc., the reform of education and giving new life to language and literature.[1]

Gandhian ideology which pervaded the contemporary political scene had a tremendous impact on Indian writing in English, in general, and Indian English fiction, in particular:

> Gandhiji is not only an Indo-Anglian writer in his own right but a colossus who bestrides almost over the entire field of Indian writing in English in several forms, appearing either as a character or as a subject or as a pervasive influence upon the social and political scene depicted by the writer.[2]

K.S. Venkataramani, Mulk Raj Anand, Raja Rao, R.K. Narayan, Bhabani Bhattacharya, Nagarajan, Nayantara Sahgal, Kamala Markandaya and Manohar Malgonkar gave expression in their fictional writings to the impact of Gandhi on the masses and the freedom struggle led by him.

K.S. Venkataramani's *Murugan, the Tiller* can be described as a treatise on Gandhian economics. He describes how many Indians relinquished their glittering posts and became followers of Gandhi. In his *Kandan, the Patriot* the major characters are inspired by Gandhian ideals and social reforms. The image of Gandhi as presented by Venkataramani is one of an agrarian reformer.

Though he does not have much faith in Gandhian political ideology, Mulk Raj Anand is impressed by Gandhi's genuine interest in the welfare of the downtrodden. He introduces Gandhi as a character in *Untouchable*. In *The Sword and the Sickle*, Anand shows how Lalu, the protagonist, though impressed by Gandhi's peasant-like appearance and sincerity, refuses to be convinced of the effectiveness of Gandhi's non-violent struggle. The irreverent remarks of Lalu and other revolutionaries on Gandhi reflect Anand's attitude to Gandhi's non-violent struggle. Both in *Untouchable* and *The Sword and the Sickle*, Anand questions the effectiveness of Gandhian solution to the problems of untouchables and the peasants.

In Raja Rao's *Kanthapura*, we find, perhaps, the finest picture of Gandhi's impact on rural India. Though Gandhi does not appear as a character, the novel shows how "the whirlwind of Gandhian revolution" shakes a South Indian village to its roots. Raja Rao successfully depicts how "Gandhi tapped the deeply religious and spiritual resources of our people living in the remotest parts of India and built up a national movement in one life-time."[3] In *The Cow of the Barricades*, Raja Rao reveals how Gandhi wanted India to be a land of peace with an unswerving faith in 'ahimsa.'

In Bhabani Bhattacharya's *So Many Hungers!* Gandhi stands for love, truth and non-violence. This is driven home to us through Devesh Basu, a typical Gandhian, with his wholehearted commitment to village reconstruction. Manjeri S. Isvaran's "Between Two Flags" reveals how even youngsters fearlessly jumped into the freedom struggle inspired by Gandhi. Thus, the image of Gandhi projected in the pre-Independence Indian English fiction is an ideal image barring Mulk Raj Anand's note of dissent.

The post-Independence Indian English novelists who treat Gandhi in their fiction seem to take their cue from Anand and present Gandhi in realistic terms rather than on an idealistic plane. Though K.A. Abbas presents Gandhi in *Inqilab* as an apostle of non-violence and votary of Hindu-Muslim unity, he seems to believe more in Jawaharlal Nehru as the future hope of India. This is made clear to us through Anwar, who though an admirer of Gandhi, is chilled by the religious aspect of Gandhi's satyagraha.

Although R.K. Narayan does not present Gandhi in his characteristic ironic vision in his *Waiting for the Mahatma*, he shows how Gandhian ideology has not been properly understood even by his close followers like Sriram and how Gandhi's name is exploited by people like Natesh, the Municipal Chairman, for their own selfish ends. In *The Vendor of Sweets*, R.K. Narayan goes a step further by caricaturing the present-day Gandhians like Jagan who poses and pretends to follow Gandhi. In his *Chronicles of Kedaram,* Nagarajan presents Gandhi as one who offers a healing touch to the feuding factions and, at the same time, like R.K.Narayan, he shows how pseudo-followers of Gandhi like Vanchi exploit him to further their interests.

After nearly five decades of writing, Mulk Raj Anand once again introduces Gandhi as a character in *Little Plays of Mahatma Gandhi*. Anand presents Gandhi as a humanist par excellence. The passing of forty-nine years has evidently brought about a perceptible change in Anand's attitude to Gandhi. Azad, the protagonist of the novel, who refuses to call Gandhi Bapu in the beginning, touches his feet and seeks his blessings before leaving the ashram. Azad leaves the ashram with the conviction that Gandhian humanism is the panacea for all the ills of the society.

Of all the Indian writers who have used Gandhi for their creative purposes, Chaman Nahal is the most significant. No one has written so extensively on Gandhi as Nahal. *The Gandhi Quartet* successfully reconstructs the three phases of India's struggle for freedom—the non-cooperation movement of 1920-22, the civil disobedience movement of 1930-31 and the Quit India movement of 1942. It also gives a moving account of the division of India into India and Pakistan, and the disaster that follows it. Nahal portrays nearly two hundred characters representing different ethnic groups and the enigmatic personality of Gandhi. Taken as a single entity, *The Gandhi Quartet* constitutes the most extensive Commonwealth novel.

The Crown and the Loincloth narrates the conflict between the British government represented by the crown and national movement for freedom led by Gandhi, represented by loincloth. It projects Gandhi at the macro level and Sunil at the micro level. Nahal vindicates the nobility of non-violence over terrorism by making Sunil sacrifice his life while trying to save the Prince of Wales.

The Salt of Life concerns itself with Gandhi's epoch-making Dandi March of 1930. Nahal narrates how Kusum, "a devoted follower" of Gandhi, marries Raja Vishal Chand and leaves Gandhi's Ashram, while Vikram, her son by Sunil, stays behind with Gandhi. Vikram, though young, walks with Gandhi to Dandi and breaks the Salt Law. After the Raja's death, Kusum returns to Gandhi.

The Triumph of the Tricolour deals with the Quit India movement. It also narrates the rise of Subhas Bose and the violent revolutionaries "in the challenge to the British rule." Amit, Kusum's son by Raja Vishal Chand, joins the revolutionaries while Vikram is inclined towards the Gandhian path. Vikram refuses to accept office in the interim government. Instead, he joins Gandhi in the latter's efforts to offer healing touch to the victims of communal frenzy.

Azadi which is devoted to India's partition is "neither a romantic nor a political tale, but an intensely moving human saga of displacement and loss of identity."[4] Nahal describes in detail the detestable inhuman acts committed both by the Hindus and Muslims against one another. The harrowing events associated with the partition are presented mainly through the family and friends of Lala Kanshi Ram of Sialkot. They lose everything including the ability to communicate. During their journey to Delhi, they are shocked to see how "a section of humanity occasionally lapse into a wild and barbaric state of mind and betray their heritage by inexplicably indulging in fiendish behaviour towards their fellowmen less powerfully placed."[5]

The "Epilogue" at the end of *Azadi* successfully connects all the four volumes of *The Gandhi Quartet*. It gives none-too-happy but true picture of post-Independence India. In the end, Nahal seems to suggest that a return to Gandhi is the only solution to the problems people face today. The "Epilogue" to *Azadi*, like Shaw's "Epilogue" to *Saint Joan*, forms an integral part of *The Gandhi Quartet*.

II

Chaman Nahal is as much a historian as a novelist because *The Gandhi Quartet* is a fictionalization of the three phases of India's struggle for freedom, "the ecstasy of Independence, the agony of the partition and the bathos of post-Independence fumbling." As Jeremy Hawthorn says: "the historical novel sets its events and characters in a well-defined historical context, and it may include both fictional and real characters. It is often distinguished (in its more respectable forms) by convincing detailed description of the manners, building, institutions and scenery of its chosen setting, and generally attempts to convey a sense of historical verisimilitude."[6]

Chaman Nahal's *The Gandhi Quartet* narrates the historical events between 1920 and 1952. The first novel, *The Crown and the Loincloth* is about the non-violent non-cooperation movement of 1920. The second novel, *The Salt of Life* narrates Gandhi's historic march to Dandi in 1930. *The Triumph of the Tricolour*, the third novel, deals with the Quit India movement of 1942 and the formation of the interim government in 1946. The fourth novel, *Azadi*, describes how the British liquidate their 'Raj' in India by dividing India into two countries on the basis of religion and the tragedy that follows the division of the subcontinent in 1947. The process of selection of the three phases in India's struggle for freedom and the partition of India reveals Nahal's skill as a historical novelist. It lends sense of fullness and prevents the novel from being "cluttered with trivial journalistic details." Nahal depicts the historical personages—Gandhi, Jawaharlal Nehru, Subhas Bose, Jinnah, Bhagat

Singh, Dyer, Mountbatten and Kasturbai. However, *The Gandhi Quartet* is not merely a composition of a series of past incidents reproduced with literal fidelity. The plot includes private incidents also—the fortunes of the members of the fictional families of Thakur Shanti Nath of Ajitha and Lala Kanshi Ram of Sialkot. Though the fictional characters operate at their own level, almost all of them come under the influence of the towering personality of Gandhi. In fact, Gandhi with his multifaceted personality dwarfs everyone around him. However, Nahal does not make Gandhi the protagonist of *The Gandhi Quartet.* As he says, "Gandhi did not lend himself to a romantic and glamourized treatment. . . . The fictional story that I had wanted to spin around him would have to be a fictional story about fictional and somewhat minor characters alone."[7]

The most challenging task a historical novelist faces is the interaction of historical and fictional characters. Nahal admirably succeeds in this. Sunil, the protagonist of *The Crown and the Loincloth*, impressed by Gandhian ideology, works for the uplift of the untouchables and in the end dies while trying to save the Prince of Wales. Then, his wife, Kusum, joins Gandhi in his ashram. In *The Salt of Life*, the young Vikram, son of Kusum and Sunil, becomes a follower of Gandhi and takes part in the Salt Satyagraha. After the death of her second husband, Raja Vishal Chand, Kusum returns to Gandhi's ashram. On Bapu's advice, she leads satyagraha against the oppressive regime. *The Triumph of the Tricolour* shows how Amit, son of Kusum and Raja Vishal Chand, works in tandem with Vikram for the freedom of the motherland. After the assassination of Gandhi, Vikram shuns power and decides to carry on the work that was dear to Gandhi. *Azadi* narrates how Lala Kanshi Ram's daughter, Madhu, married to the grandson of Thakur Shantinath, is butchered by communalists. Then, Lala Kanshi Ram with his wife, son and thousands of other refugees marches to Delhi in search of identity. Thus, *The Gandhi Quartet* is a synthesis of the historical events affecting individual lives and of individual lives significantly manifesting the forces at work in society during 1915 and 1952.

That *The Gandhi Quartet* is free from anachronisms goes to

prove that Nahal has done a great amount of research into the periods between 1915 and 1952. He is accurate in giving the details of the period, description of people, their mode of speech, food habits and other features. Nahal successfully recreates the milieu of the period of the story.

Nahal uses history as a handmaiden to achieve several purposes. In *The Gandhi Quartet*, he strives to educate and entertain the readers and discuss day-to-day problems: "It is in the historical novel only that day-to-day problems of life can be encountered, examined, exposed, challenged and rectified. Entertainment and instruction are, by common consent, the most valued virtues of historical fiction."[8]

Through his portrayal of Kusum and Abha, Nahal seems to challenge the archetypal image of the wife and woman in the patriarchal society. He asks: "After all, in the well-being of a marriage why should the woman alone make sacrifices, why not the man too."[9] Kusum refuses to pardon Sunil, her husband, for having fallen in love with Rehna. After Sunil's death, she violates the ashram vows, and sleeps with Raja Vishal Chand because the latter brings delight into her life. She, in turn, extends "restorative sustenance" to the Raja.

Nahal's depiction of the character, Abha, clearly reveals that Nahal is an advocate of feminism. He defines feminism as "a mode of existence in which the woman is free of the dependence syndrome. There is a dependence syndrome; whether it is the husband or the father or the community or whether it is a religious group, ethnic group. When women free themselves of the dependence syndrome and lead a normal life, my idea of feminism materializes."[10] Abha succeeds in emancipating herself from the claustrophobic enclosures and dependency syndrome and decides to lead an independent life as a doctor. Later, she even defies religious heads and adopts a child. Thus, a study of *The Gandhi Quartet* shows that Nahal succeeds in "combining politics with the best aspects of the estheticism of the fifties, particularly in terms of the formal aspects of writing: plot structure, innovative narrative techniques, complexity of characterization, a new *versimo* in dialogue, etc."[11]

III

However, Nahal is not free from certain lapses and bias as a historical novelist using the technique of the Quartet. For instance, in *The Salt of Life*, after meeting Bhagat Singh in the Lahore Central Jail, Nehru thinks that if the former

> was guilty of cognizable offences he must suffer the punishment for those offences. In the last run, the violent revolutionaries, having made the gestures they wanted, hoped to be saved—for further revolutionary action perhaps. This is where the Gandhian methods differed. Gandhi insisted that he and his associates be given the maximum punishment possible for the laws they were breaking. (82)

There was no evidence whatsoever to prove that Bhagat Singh had ever made an appeal either to Gandhi or to any other member of the Congress to save his life. On the other hand, there is sufficient documentary evidence to show that Gandhi in spite of being pressurized by many young people to plead for the life of Bhagat Singh, disregarded their appeal. Bhagwan Josh writes: "The Karachi Congress was meeting under the shadow of great tragedy. The youth of the country felt very strongly that Gandhi had not served the cause of nationalism by concluding a pact with the government which did not include the communication of Bhagat Singh's death sentence."[12]

From August 9, 1942, onwards, there were two sets "Quit India" and "Do or die." They are usually attributed to Gandhi and the Congress. Nahal does the same. But Satyavrata Ghosh writes:

> 'Do or die' was the resolution taken by the group of young revolutionaries who had attacked and captured the Chittagong armouries.
>
> In 1938, Subhas Chandra Bose was the first to demand, at the Bengal Provincial Conference at Jalpaiguri, that the British should quit India. He was then the Congress president. . . . Bose wanted the Congress to give a

> six-month ultimatum to the British to leave the country.[13]

A study of *The Crown and the Loincloth* shows that Nahal is biased against the Marxist revolutionaries. He writes;

> These young male revolutionaries made such an impact on girls when they talked of dialectical materialism, the bourgeoisie, and the proletariat. They used vocabulary that had never figured in the girls' minds and the poor creatures were swept clean off their feet. . . . Marxism might or might not succeed in India, but Marxism would have played the greatest role in the introduction of free love in the country. The girls abandoned all ties and ran away with the revolutionaries. Posing as cousins. Yet sleeping with them and talking of Marx. There was a mushroom of man-woman teams going round the country generating political sedition during the day and sexual sedition during the night. (379)

But the following lines written by G. Adhikari show that Nahal's remarks against the Marxists are uncalled for.

> In the year 1926, the central leadership of the Communist Party of India formed at the first communist conference held in Kanjar on 26-27 December 1925 took the initial steps to begin mass activity in the trade-union movement and in the national freedom movement.[14]

It is evident from these lines that there was no Marxist Party as such before 1925. So Nahal is not justified in his attack on the Marxists.

Chaman Nahal contradicts himself within his novel, *Azadi*. While writing about the Hindus and Muslims living together in Sialkot, he writes: "there was utter harmony between them." (54) But he has already revealed that they have been killing one another for many months. (41) Later, he writes: "It was only during the last year they had formed a youth club to face the Muslims." (71)

Nahal seems to indulge in contradiction in his description of man-woman relationship in *The Gandhi Quartet*. He says:

> The situation regarding the treatment of women in Indian English fiction is so anachronistic that the pleasure principle in man-woman relationship is completely abjured by the Indian novelist. . . . That marriage or love or sexual relationships can give joy and happiness as well, is ignored by most of our novelists. That's why I would laud another recently published novel in India. *The Song of Anasuya* (1978) by Uma Vasudev, a novel that has been relegated by most Indian critics to "erotica." This is perhaps the only Indian English novel in which a woman is shown having an orgasm and enjoying it.[15]

The following passage from *The Salt of Life* expounds Nahal's belief in the pleasure principle in man-woman relationship:

> The man whispered, 'Please! Oh, Please!' and opening her blouse, took her breast in his mouth. 'My God, my God!' she cried in a hoary voice. 'I'm not your mother,' she whispered close to his ear. 'You are everything. My mother, my beloved.' . . . And her legs parted to receive him into her womb . . . and as he went inside, she uttered a long drawn out moan. 'Ah,' she cried out. 'Oh,' she moaned.
>
> There was no remorse in her as she sat later on the couch and Raja Vishal Chand offered apologies. (85)

However, the same cannot be said of the following passages. In *The Triumph of the Tricolour*, while narrating how in certain Indian homes, a married woman is considered the common property, a woman writes:

> My husband has three older and two younger brothers. And all five of them have had their way with me. They keep waiting outside the door in a line and the moment their brother, that's my husband is out of sight, they jump

> into my bed. They don't even allow me to wipe or clean myself. One after another they just pummel me. (316)

Again while describing Shalini, a tribal girl, who is being readied as a bride in their traditional way, Nahal writes in the "Epilogue": "The betel nut fell directly on the opening of her flame, capping and crowning it. While rubbing against her flame, it would set it burning, preparing her further for the man who would be going into her." (316)

It cannot be denied that these passages serve sex interest of the readers. Though "it is now accepted as a literary convention to be utterly outspoken on sexual matters," K.R. Srinivasa Iyengar says: "I have my reservations about the need for the intrusion of so many sex situations and descriptions and perhaps more of suggestion and less of elaboration and explicitness may have served the purpose even better."[16]

While writing about Nahal's portrayal of Madhu and her brother, Arun, Mohan Jha observes: "The sort of openness that is exhibited in relation to Madhu and Arun verges almost on incest which does violence to our sense of propriety."[17]

Nahal's lengthy description of how Aunt Celia spends a lot of time teaching many things to the dog, Spindle, in *The Crown and the Loincloth* is welcome as a satire on one of the fads of the rich people. However, one feels that the following lines written about the dog should have been avoided:

> Spindle dashed out as if his bladder were filled to bursting. Yet when he was about to raise his leg near a bush in the lawn, his attention would be diverted . . . she (aunt Celia) didn't have a whole day to spare for Spindle—no, she had not a moment. But Spindle simply wouldn't urinate. (170)

IV

But these limitations and lapses in *The Gandhi Quartet* are easily outweighed by numerous merits. One of the chief merits of *The Gandhi Quartet* is its flavour of India in general and the

Punjab in particular. Along with national events, Nahal gives a faithful account of the social scene of the Punjab of the 1920s, 30s, and 40s which is marked by religious harmony among the Hindus, Sikhs and Muslims. Their unity is manifested in the communal sit-down meal during which they exchange sallies. Nahal reveals the bonds of friendship that exist between different families by describing how the families of Sunil and Muzaffar Ahmad gather every evening at Muzaffar's house. They spend their time sharing food, discussing various things and exchanging riddles. The affinity that exists among them is revealed in the way they address one another. Arun addresses Ghani as "uncle Ghani" and the latter greets Arun with the words "ohai, Arun 'de puter,' how're you?"

In *The Triumph of the Tricolour*, Nahal gives a beautiful and vivid description of the holy city of Banaras with its temples along its ghats, 'pandas' squatting under the palm-leaf umbrellas and helping the pilgrims in offering prayers:

> The holy city is vibrant throughout the year—pilgrims come from as far as Travancore in the south, Sindh in the west, Kashmir in the north, and Assam in the east. . . . And once in twelve, the crowds swell to over a million. These are the Kumbhs, when the Ganges is the holiest ever. (63)

Nahal's detailed account of the marriage ceremony of Amit and Shalini, a tribal girl, helps us to have a glimpse of the various customs of the tribals, the way they dress, and their superstitions. For instance, in the "Epilogue," they make the bride and bridegroom sit in two different baskets and carry them to the marriage ceremony:

> Two of the youngsters lifted the basket as though it contained nothing and easily hoisted it over their shoulders. . . . Shalini and Amit exchanged the garlands to a general shout and loud blowing of the trumpets. In another swoop, they exchanged the rings. (346-54)

Nahal reveals the unique sense of solidarity that existed among the Indians in the pre-partition days. They respond to Gandhi's call as one and take part in the three mass movements. Nahal also describes how the partition divides the one people into Hindus and Muslims and how sense of otherness replaces sense of togetherness immediately after the partition. At Amritsar, Lala Kanshi Ram feels humiliated to learn that the train carrying Muslim refugees to Pakistan is stopped and hundreds of them are massacred. But many Indian refugees joyfully shout "Serves them right."

A striking feature of *The Gandhi Quartet* is the variety of themes. The theme of *The Crown and the Loincloth* is the clash between British imperialism and Indian nationalism on one hand, and non-violent resisters and violent revolutionaries on the other. *The Salt of Life* has for its themes the Salt Satyagraha led by Gandhi, the movements led by Bhagat Singh and Subhas Bose and women's emancipation. The theme of *The Triumph of the Tricolour* is the Quit India movement. The dismemberment of India in 1947 and the horrific incidents that followed partition form the theme of *Azadi*.

The plot of each novel is handled in its own way based on the theme of the novel concerned. The plots of *The Salt of Life* and *Azadi* are woven round Gandhi, Kusum and Lala Kanshi Ram respectively. In *The Crown and the Loincloth* the plot moves round Gandhi, Sunil and Rakesh and in *The Triumph of the Tricolour* round Gandhi, Kusum, Vikram and Amit. Nahal arranges his material in such a way that the plot of each novel has an analyzable form and meaning.

Nahal succeeds in delineating convincingly all the principal historical and fictional characters. The characters in *The Gandhi Quartet* represent various shades of human nature: "To say that there are different types of characters is to say in effect that the novelists use characters and character portrayals for a range of different purposes."[18]

Lala Kanshi Ram is heroic and composed and Chaudhri Barkat Ali composed. Abdul Ghani and Captain Rahmat-Ullah Khan represent the wicked and devilish. Sunil and Vikram stand for the "confessedly ordinary" who under the impact of Gandhi become heroic, shun power and fame and choose to propagate and implement the ideals that are dear to Bapu. Nahal's women characters also represent different shades of human nature. Kusum, Sunanda and Abha are so resolute that they rise above their misfortunes, discover their true selves and make affirmations.

For characterization, Nahal adopts not only the older telling method but makes an effective use of dramatic or showing method. He makes use of both the telling method and dramatic method while delineating the character of Abha. Gandhi's personality is revealed through methods like description, conversation, action, reveries and internal monologue. His description of Gandhi just before the latter begins the second mass movement in *The Salt of Life* makes the readers feel that they are seeing Gandhi before them:

> a frail man of sixty, five feet by four inches in height, wearing metal framed spectacles with round glasses, a man with large ears, spindly legs, long arms and hands, his head cropped close and with many of his front teeth missing, a dark man in a loincloth of handspun khadi, a pocket watch dangling by his side, a staff in his hand, not to steady himself but to affirm his bearing as an ascetic. (175)

The Gandhi Quartet is replete with similar passages. They clearly reveal the impact of the pre-Raphaelite poets on Chaman Nahal. For retrospective evaluation of Gandhi's struggle in South Africa, Nahal resorts to the technique of reveries. Gandhi's conversation with the two girl inmates of the Tolstoy Farm, Harilal, Laxmidas, Kallenbach and Mir Alam are meant for a dramatic portrayal of Gandhi's personality.

Nahal opines that the Indian character can truly be rendered only if the writer gets close enough to the way an Indian thinks: "Can't diaries, letters, monologues be interspersed in it? . . . The Indian narrative has to be a combine of all the different forms of story-telling available to us."[19]

Accordingly, Nahal, perhaps for the first time in Indian

English fiction, introduces the narrative devices of diaries to reveal Abha's character, and letters to expose the different views of the people to the brutal murders in *The Triumph of the Tricolour*. Apart from these two narrative techniques, what makes Nahal unique as a novelist is his penchant for writing long sentences. For instance, to narrate Kusum's thoughts on seeing Amit and Shalini as bride and bridegroom, Nahal writes a sentence running into nine pages in "Epilogue" to *Azadi* (355-63).

Nahal's employment of the fictional devices like irony, symbol, conflict and contrast merit critical attention. His use of irony is particularly telling:

> In *Azadi*, Tagore's poem—'Where the mind is without fear'—which is prefixed to the novel, provides a powerful ironic lens to look at the meaning of the novel. The 'heaven of freedom' envisaged by the poet-sage in the poem constantly rings in the reader's mind as he goes on to witness how freedom remained 'a wiped-out dream' and 'a false dawn of freedom' at political, social, religious and personal levels.[20]

To cite one more example, Dyer almost beats the life out of Sunil hoping that it would wean the latter away from Gandhi. But it only strengthens Sunil's resolve to become a true follower of Gandhi and in the end he dies while trying to save the Prince of Wales, the symbol of the alien government.

Nahal's use of symbols, especially in *Azadi*, is significant. The titles of the three parts of *Azadi*, are "Lull," "Storm," and "Aftermath." Sea is the dominant symbol which runs through the three parts of the novel: "from the lull of suspense and stupor the novel gets into the storm of communal orgy that leaves its visible impact, as aftermath, on the last part of the book."[21]

Kurukshetra is another symbol denoting the war that was believed to have been fought between the same countrymen. The vultures that chase Kusum in *The Triumph of the Tricolour* symbolize communal hatred that results in senseless and brutal killings of one's own countrymen. In *The Crown and the Loincloth* the crown denotes the oppressive and unwanted British regime and the loincloth suggests Gandhi. When Gandhi is sentenced to six years's imprisonment, Nahal says "the lion in the loincloth was caged."

Nahal makes an exquisite use of the stylistic devices of contrast and conflict. In *Azadi* the "demonic creatures" Abdul Ghani, Inayat-Ullah Khan and Captain Rahmat-Ullah Khan offer a contrast with Bill Davidson, Chaudhri Barkat Ali and the Hakim, who are sympathetic and enlightened. Gangu Mull, who becomes a Muslim so that he can remain in the newly created Pakistan and retain his property, is contrasted with Niranjan Singh, who is steadfast in his faith.

The Gandhi Quartet narrates mainly the conflict between the colonizer and the nationalists fighting to make the former quit India on the one hand and non-violence and terrorism on the other. It also presents the conflict between Thakur Shantinath who believes in the joint family system and his children and grandchildren who like to lead independent lives.

There are parallels between events and descriptions. The Hindus undergo different types of suffering during their "long-drawn and arduous trek" from Sialkot to Dera Baba Nanak at the hands of the Muslims. The Muslims in their turn undergo similar tragic experiences before they reach Pakistan. In *The Triumph of the Tricolour*, Nahal describes Banaras thus: "The holy city of Banaras has temples along its ghats, and bells tinkling in those temples, and prayers going on." (162) After a while, he calls the same "The unholy city" because of the narrow lanes and "the mire and the mud" and filth that would make one faint. The presentation of contrasts and parallels reveal the author's non-commitment and objective view.

A study of *The Gandhi Quartet* clearly shows that Nahal has tried to mould English into a suitable medium for realistic representation of life in India. He does it by making a free use of whole sentences translated from the regional language, free use of riddles from Punjabi language and using Indian nominatives of address. For instance, in *The Triumph of the Tricolour* the traditional "tappa" sung by Darbara Singh and Naval Singh is translated into English. They sing:

Ohai, the thin one was laid easily.
But the fat one was left in the raw. . . .
Ballai, ballai. Ballai, ballai. (305)

In *Azadi*, the verse Captain Rahmat-Ullah Khan recites from Ghalib is also translated into English: "I wish I could perish before her doorstep. But she would tell me not, nor sheath her dagger." (190)

Nahal makes a freer use of the words like "Rani Sahiba," the "Yuvraj Sahib," "Chacha," "mamiji," "behanji" because they reveal reverence and affection one has for one's elders and superiors.

Solving a riddle is highly entertaining. So it becomes one of the pastimes for people. Nahal gives a few examples of such riddles in *The Gandhi Quartet*. To cite but one example from *The Crown and the Loincloth*. Rehna tells Sunil and Muzaffar that the answer for the riddle

Running fast, I fall.
Standing still, I fly in the skies (159)

is neither "the peacock" nor "an old man's beard," but "the eternal lover."

At times Nahal writes sentences spoken in the native tongue using the English alphabet. In *Azadi* we come across such sentences as

Lalaji, 'thik hai?'
'Han sahib, thik hun. Bilkul thik hun sahib.' (23)

Nahal's diction is one of the important features of his language. In *The Crown and the Loincloth*, Shyama speaks broken and faulty English because she is not well educated. True to his style of writing and speaking, Gandhi's English is remarkably simple. For instance, soon after the formation of the interim government, he says:

I must clearly tell you that the Tricolour has not triumphed

> here and in my opinion is not likely to triumph, either. . . . We are such a divided nation. Divided on race. Divided on religion. Divided on caste. . . . The India of my dreams has no place for fissures in it. (486)

While giving the portrait of Sunanda in *Azadi*, Nahal's language turns lyrical: "She walked with majesty even in grief, and floated out into the street like a tableau." (154)

The Gandhi Quartet is sprinkled with gentle humour, fun and satire. Gandhi goes to the hut of Veru, a sweeper, to watch a bitch lay litter. This is noticed by the press and the next day one of the newspapers carries the news item with the caption, "Gandhi gives birth to five pups." When Griffith and his team of officials go to Mohalla Ballimaran to collect war fund, the residents make fun of them punning on the word 'chanda' which means contribution and the proper name Chanda. As an example of satire, Nahal's delineation of the Eurasians may be cited. For instance, Glady Mitchell, a nurse, is unwilling to marry an Indian as she is a Eurasian and no European comes forward to marry her because she is not a European.

A remarkable characteristic of Nahal, the novelist, is affirmation of life. He seems to agree with Bhabani Bhattacharya who stated: "I don't have a commitment with a slant. I am only committed to the affirmation of life. Life consists in taking on the challenges. I am essentially an affirmationist."[22] Nahal seems to believe that with all its ups and downs life is worth living and the path of reconciliation and readjustment, the most promising path. Gandhi, Sunil, Kusum, Lala Kanshi Ram, Arun and Sunanda "stand for the positive values of life" and they make an earnest effort to make life meaningful. Though the news of his sister, Madhu's death shocks Arun, he thinks of "the continuity of life." Lala Kanshi Ram, soon after stepping on the Indian soil, realizes that evil as well as good is present everywhere. So he decides not to hate the Muslims. After Sunil's death in *The Crown and the Loincloth,* Kusum makes her affirmation by joining Gandhi with her son, Vikram:

> She had lived only for her husband so far, she wanted to

> live for a cause now. . . . She was not only offering herself to the nation, she was offering her little son as well. (461)

V

A study of *The Gandhi Quartet* reveals that Nahal succeeds in his attempt to chronicle the modern heroic age which is usually identified with Gandhi and how under his impact, his followers like Kusum, Sunil, and Vikram are transformed from the ordinary to the heroic. Gandhi firmly believes: "all men had the inner capacity to remould themselves to be strong willed; to be fearless and death-defying; to be true Satyagrahis."[23] He brilliantly succeeds in rallying the masses round him in his struggle against the British, despite their repressive measures. He makes the people realize the need to end political subjection through non-violent measures because he is aware that

> it was not difficult for this state to neutralize and contain those forces which either followed the strategy of constitutional opposition (pre-Gandhian phase of the Congress) or attempted to evolve an insurrectionary strategy to overthrow the British rule (the revolutionary insurrectionists of Bengal, later on Ghadar Party and Bhagat Singh and finally the Communists). Gandhi succeeded in avoiding these two pitfalls of constitutionalist politics and insurrectionary politics and evolved a new paradigm to confront the colonial state—the paradigm of peaceful mass movements.[24]

Gandhi was more concerned than any other leader with the welfare of untouchables. While he was prepared even to sacrifice his life in the process of eradicating untouchability, "Jawaharlal Nehru, Gandhi's political heir, complained that the Mahatma was, "choosing a side issue for his final sacrifice!" [25]

Gandhi's loving regard for the masses and his selfless devotion to their cause, make them repose unwavering faith in him. As a result, even in his absence they take part in the Quit India movement without any fear of repercussions:

> The essential secret of the Mahatma's power over the Indian people is this. The power of the people lay repressed, dormant and stunted within their beings. When the love of the Mahatma flowed into the masses their own power was stimulated out of a wretched langour. And, in passionate gratitude they let their exuberating power of which he was the inspiration flow back to him.[26]

Nahal narrates how Gandhi gave a new interpretation to accepted Hindu notions of feminity and succeeded in making women also become active political and social agents in the freedom movement. He asked them: "to develop talents they were best suited to: they were to spin, rear their children in the spirit of 'swadeshi,' non-violence and 'dharma.'"[27] It is gratifying to note that today women are

> Mobilizing themselves on a range of ecological, political and social issues . . . are looking once more to Gandhian alternatives and to his view of religious and social tolerance . . . by using effectively proven tools of social and political protest, women are becoming an influential force in specific areas.[28]

Nahal shows how Gandhi looked "plain and ordinary" with his short stature and lean body and with rather common features. But Nahal also shows how, in spite of these physical handicaps, Gandhi becomes "a symbol of moral and spiritual strength" triumphing over his physical odds: "By associating himself with politics, he moderates and humanizes them. I should rather say he 'divinizes' them, as the 'human' left to itself is not far from the animal."[29]

Chaman Nahal's diligence, inspired objectivity and his detachment make him present not only Gandhi's "spiritual splendour, moral luminosity" but also "political warts and personal failings of which the Mahatma was only too well aware."[30] Nahal describes at length Gandhi's failure to judge people's inability to remain non-violent in the thick of the agitation. In spite of his vow of celibacy, he cannot help looking at Kasturbai with desire. Nahal also shows Gandhi as impulsive. The violent incidents at Chauri Chaura and other places in the wake of the non-cooperation movement make Gandhi sad. Concluding that he is not pure enough to make the countrymen remain non-violent in *The Crown and the Loincloth,* he thinks of committing suicide:

> "Ba, I'm going to kill myself tomorrow morning," he said, fully awake and alert. . . . "I'm not pure enough and I know no other means of making myself purer." (368)

Nahal gives a moving picture of how Gandhi, even before India gained independence, becomes a disillusioned man because of the growing indifference of the Congress intellectuals to his programme of non-violence and khadi. When Pethick-Lawrence asks Gandhi in *The Triumph of the Tricolour* whether he would accept the proposals of the Cabinet Mission, Gandhi says:

> "That's for the Congress to decide," he said, going into his proverbial smile. "I'm nobody in the Congress." (429)

In the end, his failure to wean Jinnah away from his two-nation theory and the disaster that followed partition break the heart of the apostle of peace:

> the second [non-violent action] was to Gandhi himself a failure, as independence was accompanied by partition and communal frenzy because India had accepted non-violence as a policy and not as a creed.[31]

Thus, Nahal presents a deeply realistic, highly convincing and an unusually candid portrayal of Gandhi in *The Gandhi Quartet.*

NOTES

1. K.R. Srinivasa Iyengar, *Indian Writing in English* (1962; Bombay: Asia, 1973), p. 258.

2. M.K. Naik, "Gandhiji and Indian Writing in English, *Critical Essays on Indian Writing in English*, ed. M.K. Naik et al (1968, Madras: Macmillan, 1977), p. 370.
3. C.D. Narasimhaiah, "Raja Rao's *Kanthapura*: An Analysis," *Critical Essays on Indian Writing in English*, ed. M.K. Naik et al, p. 248.
4. K. Venkata Reddy, "The Achievement of Chaman Nahal," *Critical Studies in Commonwealth Literature* (New Delhi: Prestige, 1994), p. 165.
5. K.S. Dhillon, "Depths of Depravity." rev. of *Orphans of the Storm: Stories on the Partition of India*, ed. Saros Cowasjee and K.S. Duggal, *The Book Review*, 19.5 (1995), p. 30.
6. Jeremy Hawthorn, *Studying the Novel: An Introduction* (New Delhi: Universal Book Stall, 1992), pp. 15-16.
7. Chaman Nahal, "Writing a Historical Novel," *Three Contemporary Novelists*, ed. R.K. Dhawan (New Delhi: Classical, 1985), pp. 42-44.
8. R.K. Dhawan, "The Artist as a Historian," *Three Contemporary Novelists*, p. 3.
9. Chaman Nahal, "Second Generation of Indian English Novelists," *The New Literatures in English* (New Delhi: Allied, 1985), p. 102.
10. Chaman Nahal, "Feminism in English Fiction: Forms and Variations," *Feminism and Recent Fiction in English*, ed. Sushila Singh (New Delhi: Prestige, 1991), p. 17.
11. Carlo Coppola, "Politics and the Novel in India: A Perspective," *Politics and the Novel in India*, ed. Yogendra K. Mallik (New Delhi: Orient Longman, 1978), pp. 4-5.
12. Bhagwan Josh, *Struggle for Hegemony in India* (New Delhi: Sage, 1992), vol. 2, p. 269.
13. Satyavrata Ghosh, "The Birth of a Revolution," *The Illustrated Weekly of India*, 8-14 August 1992, p. 18.
14. G. Adhikari, *Documents of the History of the Communist Party of India* (New Delhi: People's Publishing House, 1978), p. 1.
15. Chaman Nahal, "Second Generation of Indian English Novelists," *The New Literatures in English*, p. 104.
16. K.R. Srinivasa Iyengar, rev. of *The Crown and the Loincloth*, *The Literary Criterion*, 16.3 (1981), p. 79.
17. Mohan Jha, "Chaman Nahal's *Azadi*: A Search for Identity," *Studies in Indian Fiction in English*, ed. G.S. Balarama Gupta (Gulbarga: JIWE, 1987), p. 44.

18. Jeremy Hawthorn, *Studying the Novel: An Introduction*, p. 49.
19. Chaman Nahal, "The Dancers in the Ring: *The Little Plays of Mahatma Gandhi*," *The Novels of Mulk Raj Anand*, ed. R.K. Dhawan (New Delhi: Prestige, 1992), p. 228.
20. K. Venkata Reddy, p. 173.
21. Mohan Jha, pp. 125-26.
22. Bhabani Bhattacharya, interview, B.S. Goyal, *Hindustan Times*, 15 Jan. 1978.
23. Bhabani Bhattacharya, *Mahatma Gandhi* (1977; New Delhi: Arnold Heinemann, 1982), p. 85.
24. Bhagwan Josh, *Struggle for Hegemony in India*, vol. 2, p. 52.
25. P. Mani, "Abstract Logical Construct: Indian History without Gandhi," *The Secret of Mahatma Gandhi: The Harmonic Counterpoint* (New Delhi: Arnold, 1989), p. 83.
26. *Ibid.*, p. 98.
27. Malavika Karlekar, "The Return of Mohandas Karamchand Gandhi: A Comparative Perspective," *Indian Journal of Gender Studies*, 2.1 (1995), p. 52.
28. *Loc. cit.*
29. Romain Rolland, "Letter to Kalidas Nag," *Selected Letters of Romain Rolland*, ed. Francis Dore and Marie Laure Prevost (New Delhi: OUP, 1990), p. 63.
30. K. Natwar Singh, "No Ordinary Mortal," rev. of *The Good Boatman: A Portrait of Gandhi*, by Rajmohan Gandhi, *Frontline*, 3 Nov. 1995, p. 81.
31. S. Gopal, "A Life of Integrated Unity," rev. of *Mahatma Gandhi: Non-Violent Power in Action* by Denis Dalton, *The Book Review*, 19.4 (1995), p. 3.